Moments In Time

R.W. DOYEN
Moments In Time

ReadersMagnet, LLC

Moments In Time
Copyright © 2020 by R.W. Doyen

Published in the United States of America
ISBN Paperback: 978-1-951775-02-5
ISBN eBook: 978-1-951775-03-2

All rights reserved. No part of this publication may be reproduced, stored in a retrieval system or transmitted in any way by any means, electronic, mechanical, photocopy, recording or otherwise without the prior permission of the author except as provided by USA copyright law.

The opinions expressed by the author are not necessarily those of ReadersMagnet, LLC.

ReadersMagnet, LLC
10620 Treena Street, Suite 230 | San Diego, California, 92131 USA
1.619.354.2643 | www.readersmagnet.com

Book design copyright © 2020 by ReadersMagnet, LLC. All rights reserved.
Cover design by Ericka Obando
Interior design by Shemaryl Tampus

Prologue

Bill's father was gone now, born in 1915 he had died in the year 2000. It was plain to see that it wouldn't be so very many years that he would be gone as well. He too was getting old, at seventy-seven he was fast approaching eighty. Some things just weren't predictable. He wasn't likely to live as long or as well as his father had. If he was going to tell his story, then he had better be getting to it. His father had passed a legacy to him, one of sage advice, and a way of looking at life. It was up to him to see to it that his father's name and his deeds were not forgotten. He also wanted to acknowledge those besides his father who had helped him surmount his struggles and achieve his successes. Bill wasn't sure if the story he wanted to write would be of his father or of himself. It was confusing. Bill's early life was deeply entwined with that of his father and mentor. Like the double helix of their shared DNA, so too was the spiraled and interwoven plait of memories.

He wished, above all to share the hardships and the humor in his life with the future generations of his family.

Although those future generations will face unique challenges, unique to themselves, a common thread would exist that connected the future with the past, but only if he recorded it. Their struggles will have the weight and support of those who came before.

It would be up to him to chronicle the events, which were so important in his life, for them.

Contents

Chapter 1: The Plan 9
Chapter 2: The Interlude 27
Chapter 3: Bill's Big Break 44
Chapter 4: Into The Breach 51
Chapter 5: Night Talks 59
Chapter 6: The Long Walk 81
Chapter 7: Farm Life 89
Chapter 8: Of Moose, Paddles, And Presidents 98
Chapter 9: The Long Hard Summer 124
Chapter 10: The University, Love, And Beyond 136

Epilogue 157

Chapter 1

THE PLAN

Spots of blood highlighted angry swollen welts. Excoriation streaks ran across the back of his hands and down his arms. Circling his neck above the protection of his collar, huge red wheals from insect bites tortured his skin. Absentmindedly Bill abraded the irritating welts with his ragged chewed nails as he fought to maintain his balance. The narrow rear seat didn't offer much for him to hold onto. The little Willis Jeep slowly jounced its way over large boulders and deep ruts. His father, in the driver's seat, maneuvered the jeep along the ancient, rarely used, trail. The little four-cylinder engine would whine as the R.P.M.'S climbed and then returned to a purr as its speed subsided.

The long forgotten and neglected "tote" road had been carved from the Maine wilderness back in the mid-twenties when the last major logging operation in that area had prompted its construction. For the past twenty-five years the tangled overgrown wood roads had been only used by the occasional fisherman with a vehicle rugged enough to navigate it, or legs determined enough to walk the distance.

How things had changed. When this wild land first opened up to the woodcutters, a barracks that housed a hundred men had been built along with stables for as many horses. There were barns to store food and hay and coffee and grain; there were blacksmiths for hoofs and cobblers for feet. The hive of scurrying men and animals had been built through one short Maine summer. When cold weather blasted its way down from the north, the country was closed until spring. Once cold set in and deep snows began to accumulate, both the men and the horses were in camp for the winter. The torturous winding rough cut roads, that twisted through the mountains were seldom used in the summer. Warm weather rains would sog the roads into muddy quagmires. Washouts and deep potholes were very common. Repairs couldn't keep up with nature's wrath. No horse drawn wagon with a massive load of logs could possibly make the journey.

"Pop?" Bill finally asked. "If the roads were impassable in summer and piled deep with snow in the winter, how did they get the wood out?"

"It was an ingenious labor-intensive system, but it worked." Bill's father paused to let his memory drift back to his own youth when he saw the operation firsthand.

Bracing against the joint jarring flesh bruising roughness of the road, Bill's imagination leaped back twenty–five years, picturing the men at their labors. "When was this road built? Bill asked his father.

"I'm not sure, I was told the last job in here shut down in 1929, just after the crash. So, it's been about twenty–five years, since it was last used, but I think it was originally built in the early twenties.

Settling back into the seat, Bill entwined what he knew of the work back then with the details that his father provided.

The wilderness roads stretched through the unbroken forest for miles as the loggers cut their way into the stands of virgin timber with their axes and crosscuts.

Horses were used to drag the logs to loading areas where they were stacked. Loading areas or "yards" would be established every quarter mile or so. Once the roads were frozen over, a road crew would fill tanker wagons with water from a nearby spring or brook. The roads were then hosed down with water, and overnight, would freeze to a ribbon of ice. After each big snowstorm, the roads would be packed with giant, horse drawn rollers, and wet down again.

When everything was frozen solid the logs could be hauled out on huge horse drawn sleds with steel runners. The sleds would be off loaded onto great racked trucks at the main road and taken to the mills.

"So, Pop", asked Bill, "when the wood was all cut and hauled away the roads were all just let go?"

"Sure. They weren't needed anymore."

The forces of nature were powerful and unrelenting. The fishermen who used these slowly eroding paths to get far back off the beaten paths in their pursuit of speckled trout, for a few years after the woodcutters had left, the diehard fishermen would use the roads until they became too difficult to walk on. Some of the worst washouts would be repaired from time to time, but it was a losing battle.

The summer of 1954 was starting out to be a good one for Bill, if only the bugs would stop biting.

Bill's long journey toward his manhood began on this fishing trip into Maine's far back country. It was July of 1954 He was thirteen years old. He was suddenly jolted out of his daydreams as his seat cushion dropped out from under him in a bone jarring thud. The further from the main road they went and the closer to "C" Pond they got, the worse the rock-strewn track became. In addition to the bone abusing ride, black flies, mosquitoes, and the no-see-ums inflicted. Not even the favorite "Woodsman's Fly Dope" could stem the onslaught.

Henry Ames had been Ray's trapping partner for the past few years and was along for the day's fishing trip.

The three occupants of the jeep kept their eyes on the narrow-overgrown trail, wet from bleeding underground springs. The roadway was laced with pools that refracted the sunbeam to a cascade of colors and provided an excellent breeding pool for the millions of tiny blood-sucking bugs.

The mountain air, in spite of being mid-summer was cool and moist. The hundred shades of green surrounded and accentuated the unbroken blue of the sky above.

"I'm being eaten alive," Bill complained, "When are we going to get there?" "C" Pond was a secluded, seldom fished, body of water that lay about eight to ten miles from the nearest hard top road. The trail they were on now, in spite of the jeep, was on the verge of decay and nearly beyond the jeep's considerable might. The pond's water supply was maintained by springs, winter run-off and numerous small brooks that trickled down from the hillside. "C Pond" was the headwaters for the dead Cambridge River that eventually emptied into the Umbagog Lake across the state line in New Hampshire.

"I sure hope it's worth it," Bill said between scratching and slapping.

The two men said nothing, just grinned at each other and obviously enjoyed the discomfort of their young companion.

The little four-wheel drive vehicle continued to pound its way over and around the ruts and boulders that had been washed out and etched around by the spring run-offs and summer rains. This was hard inaccessible country, and rumor had it to be a fisherman's paradise. If true, these small inconveniences like impassable roads, biting gnats and the occasional slaps in the face from trail undergrowth, posed little problem.

Low limbs from overhanging trees had to be manually lifted above the windshield of the topless vehicle. The road looking like the dried-up bed of a mountain stream, the round water worn and possibly glacier worn cobblestone path twisted along mountainsides, over ridges and across shallow valleys.

Preparations for this trip had been made the evening before. Worms had been dug, lunches had been made, and in the morning before the haze had lifted Ray and his boy struck out. They stopped long enough to pick up Henry on their way out of town. Fifteen miles north of the small town of Mexico, the three had breezed through the tiny ancient hamlet of Andover on their way to the top of East "B" Hill. It was the jumping off point onto the trail that they now traversed on their way into "C" Pond.

Although it was now only a rutted "returning to nature" trail, the one-time road, back in the twenties, was the main artery over which tens of thousands of cords of wood were hauled to feed the paper company and the lumber yards some thirty miles away in Rumford. The going, even in the little four-wheel drive jeep, was painfully slow and occasionally the front winch was used to pull the vehicle up a steep incline, just as the specially mounted rear winch was used to slow sharp descents.

By late morning, brooks and streams feeding the Dead Cambridge River were crossed, giving hint that their destination was not far off.

"We must be getting close," Bill, said, I'm starting to see some beaver signs," Here and there through the woods the telltale signs of their gnawing could be seen. Their white conical slashings at the base of big trees lay about, with their branches missing.

"I see them "responded his father. There must be a colony or two, in these brooks leading down to the Dead Cambridge.". The branches would be dragged down to the ponds behind the dams built by the industrious rodents. The branches would be pulled into deep water and pushed into the muddy bottoms and became the stockpile of food for the coming winter.

"Well, how far Pop?" Bill asked as he dug at the rising welts forming on his exposed skin.

"It won't be long, probably not more than a mile or so," replied his father.

"You're in an awful hurry," grinned Henry, "what's the rush?"

"The flies are bleeding me dry," complained Bill, "and I want to catch some fish," he explained.

Ray was pleased with his son's excitement. He loved the woods and hoped to instill the same feelings in his young son. He knew that things were changing. The big remote woods, rich with fish and game, were being assaulted as never before by the hungry lumber and pulp mills. Huge stretches of wilderness were being carved with well-maintained roads that were being gated off. The public, with increasing frequency, was being denied access. The heritage he had grown up with, as a birth rite would be denied to his son. Ray loved to hunt, fish, and trap. He was woods wise in the old way.

Ray understood that nothing about the woods would be the same for his son as it had been for him. His era was beginning to pass. This was especially true for the beaver trapper.

Along with their habitat, the beaver population too was dwindling; trapped too hard or driven from their wilderness domain by the crush of progress. Whenever the backwater from their dams flooded across wood roads, the same roads over which the decimated forests were being hauled, then the dams were torn out or dynamited. It didn't matter a bit that the dammed-up brooks and streams were life sustaining not only for the beaver, but countless other wildlife as well. The loss of their dams and its backwater was a life-threatening disaster. It destroyed their winter homes. Many would die before spring. The senseless slaughter tore at Ray. It made him angry. He knew he could not stop or even slow the progress of their demise, even if he stopped his own trapping. Only the government's intervention or a change in style would save the beaver. For him to stop trapping beaver to save them from annihilation, he knew, would not work. It bothered him in a quiet, unspoken way that he was more a part of the problem than the solution. Should he quit trapping there would be others to take his place and the extermination would continue. Until the laws were changed to protect the beaver, he would continue the devil's work.

"We're here!" Henry's quiet exclamation jostled Ray from his deep thoughts.

"C" Pond was little more than a blue dot on a U.S. geological survey map. The rural areas of the state had been surveyed into townships. The uninhabited townships were simply designated alphabetically and "C." Pond was in C. Surplus Township.

"Thank God," muttered Bill as he jumped to the uneven ground from the back of the jeep. "I'm hungry."

"Oh, no We're not eating yet," admonished his father, "It's only about ten o'clock. We'll fish up and down along the shoreline for and get back here for lunch around one o'clock… if everyone's OK with that."

"I'm not," grinned Bill, mock consternation in his voice.

"Take a couple of candy bars out of that lunch box. That should hold you for a while." That sounded agreeable to Bill as he took his can of worms, his fly dope and his fish pole along with his candy bars and headed off to his right along the overgrown shoreline.

Branches from alder bushes overhung the shoreline and dipped into the water along the ponds edge. The water, cold and crystal clear, overlaid the soft black silty bottom. Here and there, lying in the bottom silt, could be seen the white remains of branches, stripped of their bark. Gnaw marks from beaver teeth could be seen along the shafts. Beaver didn't eat the wood, only the nutritious bark and buds along the limbs. Throughout the harsh winter the beaver would leave their domed houses, retrieve lengths of wood, bringing them up into their dens to nibble on. Once stripped bare of bark, the wood was dragged away and disposed of under the ice.

Bill was a bait caster, not having the patience or the inclination to learn the art of fly-fishing. "I want to catch fish; not see how pretty I can be while I'm doing it."

"You'll understand when you get older," his father had said. "It's no big trick to catch a fish with a worm, but the art of fly-fishing is a different thing altogether."

"Sure, Pop," said Bill in a condescending tone as he disappeared through the brush bordering the small three-acre pond that lay tucked in the cleft between two shallow ridges. He caught his father's parting advice as he crashed through the thicket of tangled branches. "If they're less than a foot-long throw um back."

"OK, Pop," he muttered, hoping that such a choice would be in the offing.

Working his way along the shoreline at times up to his waist in the near freezing spring-fed body of water, he pulled in one beautiful speckled trout after another. Doing as his father suggested, he kept only those between twelve and fourteen inches in length. Bill suspected that the natural feed for the fish may have been a bit scarce. Of the ones, he hooked, most were "6" or "7" in length and he threw them back. He managed to hook a keeper occasionally, but they were worth the trouble and the aggravation of rebating and recasting. Candy bars and hunger were soon forgotten, as the light rig, he held would jump to life in his hands.

Incredible frustration always seemed to accompany Bill when fishing in beaver ponds and the brush overgrown streams of the Maine woods. His fishing line was constantly tangled on half rotted submerged logs. Mucky unsolid ground would result in innumerable falls, sometimes up to his shoulders, in the icy water. The ever-present omnipresent blood-sucking insects paid only scant attention to the constantly reapplied fly repellant. These were but a few of the obstacles out to thwart the incredibly good time he was having.

"If it were easy, said his father, everybody would be doing it."

Over and over again he would hook into fat, strong fish that would fight gallantly to regain their freedom. Bill's pole would arch over, and the reel would zing. The rod would become alive in his hands. Being careful not to dislodge the hook, and not to play out too much line that could tangle in submerged snags, he was having the time of his life. All while slapping bugs and wiping sweat from his eyes. Carefully played, the fighting squirming prize would be brought close enough to be scooped into his net.

"Gotcha'," there was no amount of discomfort in the small world he lived that could dim this kind of excitement. By one o'clock he had made his way up and back along the shore and now stood beside his father, showing off eight of the most beautiful fish that he had ever hoped to catch.

"Where's yours, Pop?"

"I have a couple," his father answered, knowing his son would have all kinds of ridicule about fly-fishing. "You know there is a four fish limit, don't you?"

"Want some worms? I know it's not as much sport, but I get results." Bill responded ignoring his father's last comment.

"It's not that," his father retorted defensively. "Henry and I did some scouting around, up a couple of brooks over in the back," he gestured. "This place is loaded with beaver sign. We found at least five colonies in the past two hours, and I'll bet there's a dozen more if we keep looking. Most are a pretty good size, big-feed piles and a lot of water dammed up".

After lunch, Bill went back to fishing while his father and Henry spent the rest of the afternoon scouting out more beaver colonies.

Beaver are industrious bark, bud and root-eating rodents. After leaving their parents' lodge at about two years of age, they would travel cross-country or along streams in search of a new territory to set up housekeeping. When a likely spot was found they would begin building dams to create a backwater, deep enough that during the intensely cold winter, ice wouldn't freeze clear to the bottom.

On more than one occasion, Ray had found where in mid-winter a dam had given way, emptied the backwater and the beaver would either freeze or starve to death. There were other incidents too, where a lack of snow cover and severe sustained cold would freeze the beaver's pond clear to the mud. Unable to get out of their domed houses to their under-ice feed pile, they would starve to death. Fortunately, such occurrences were uncommon.

Throughout the summer the beaver along with his mate, and in many cases an extended family of last year's young, would cut an endless number of trees. It was for these tree-cutting signs that Ray and Henry searched. Extensive dam work, deep water, and big feed piles meant large colonies. As the long summer days would begin to shorten, the animals would work at a feverish pace, readying themselves for winter. As the daylight hours shrank and the temperature dipped, their winter fur would begin to thicken. Their dense undercoat would become impenetrable, even the air around the hairs could not escape, creating a dry cocoon even while submerged in frigid water. It was their pelts for which the animals were sought. The luxuriant fur had value. So much so that in times past the hides were used as currency. Contracts might have been worded, "to be paid off with 20 adult beaver hides."

Ray and Henry had stumbled into a relatively inaccessible area around "C" Pond with more beaver signs than they had ever seen before. They began to ponder the problems to overcome if they came here in the dead of winter to trap them. There was a lot of money at stake and they hoped to devise a way to get it. By midafternoon the three fishermen were back to the jeep, packed up and ready to leave. By now, their faces and arms were a mass of welts. The sun, so Maine warm in the summer, was now low in the sky. Mountain coolness could be felt through damp shirts; by six o'clock the sun would be on the rim and by seven the twilight would be giving up the day. The balminess of the afternoon air was hardly noticed, usurped by a quiet, unspoken excitement from the two men in the front seat.

From out of the blue Henry finally burst, "if we can get back in here for about a week when the season opens, we could take a lot of fur; make some serious money." Henry looked searchingly at Ray, for some kind of confirmation.

"I know," Ray responded. "We'll have to figure something out."

"What are you guys talking about?" Bill asked, leaning forward, between the two front seats.

"We're just talking. Thinking about how we're going to get back in here, and stay for a week or two, come January," his father said as he looked at his son in the rearview mirror.

"Lot of beaver in here," chimed Henry, "and we're going to figure a way to get them out."

Having trapped beaver every January since his early twenties and having spent each summer and fall searching them out, Ray was intrigued by the idea. He had trapped every pond, bog, stream and river within a half-day's ride from home; this would be a bigger challenge, but what a bonanza it could be.

Ray had learned the fine art of trapping as a young boy during the Great Depression from his uncle Luther who had a passion for trapping. He had confined his trapping to within walking distance from home, but the activity got him into the woods and helped his meager check from his job in the Oxford Paper Co.

With no children of his own, he had taken an immediate liking to the young boy. He could see that young Raymond was not intimidated by the long hours and hard labor, an integral part of trapping for fur. He enjoyed teaching the boy the little tricks needed to be successful. It was a time too when money was scarce, and he wanted the boy to get ahead.

Now in his early forties, Ray had become something of a legend in the small towns around. So cleverly could he set a trap that other trappers working the same colony would go empty handed while he would catch the entire bunch. Even trap shy adult beaver were lured into his sets.

Ray and Henry had teamed up a few years earlier when Henry approached the older man with a desire to learn how to trap. They set and tended their traps within a forty-mile radius of home. Henry learned, Ray got the help he needed, and between them were able to cover a lot more territory.

In this rural central western part of Maine there are hundreds of ponds, and a thousand miles of brooks and streams. Together they had explored and trapped much of it.

Back when Ray was young, learning from Luther, a trapper could not get much money for a beaver pelt. The country was deep in depression. Very few women wore a full-length fur coat. There was just very little market for such luxuries. By the time Ray had reached his twenties, markets had changed. Ray had discovered beaver. They were crafty, but so was he. In his quest to be the best he could be, he would not only put himself into the environment, but could strive to think as they did. Why did they build their homes where they did, and what path did they take to their underwater feed piles? He taxed his imagination and his skills. He sharpened his imagination and became one with the beaver he sought.

New York buyers would make pilgrimages to Maine several times a year to buy fur from the local buyers. When fur was the fashion, prices were good. When fashion went to cloth or leather the prices went down. Beaver coats and jackets had been the "in" thing for several years and prices had remained record high; long enough to entice anybody with the inclination, if not the skill, to try their luck. A stretched hide was measured vertically and horizontally, the two figures were added together and a prime, adult or "blanket" pelt measuring eighty or more inches would fetch a dollar or more per inch. Through the years following the depression as the country gradually became more prosperous the prices, he got for his fur steadily rose.

The trip home was relatively quiet with Bill bordering on somnolence and the two men, each lost in private thought, ruminating on the best solution to their little dilemma.

"You know, it would take us a month to set up this whole valley," said Henry.

"Shit," Ray retorted. "It may take a month, but I've only got a week that I can spare. Well two really," he continued. "A week in, to set up everything we can, a week out to get fresh supplies, and a week back in to pull the traps and bring out what we catch." For the next few miles little was said as thoughts churned. It was finally decided that Ray would call Henry after, if, he could iron out some of the details. He had a business to run and his wife, Helen, would have to run it in his absence. Knowing not to make assumptions, he would discuss his problem with her first. With a wealth of skins for the taking, it would be a shame not to get them before someone else did.

Over the next few days as plans for the great trapping expedition began to take shape, Ray would confer with his wife. She, after all, would have to run the taproom that they owned and operated. It wasn't a "businessmen on his way home from the office," kind of taproom. It was a BAR; a workingman's place to get a few drinks, and sometimes things would get out of hand. Foolish things could happen. Bad things could happen too.

Case on point was the evening Mimi Boudreau dropped by for a few drinks. By the time he came through the door, he'd already had a few—a few too many. Against his better judgment Ray served him a drink; by his second, Mimi was becoming loud and obnoxious. Not only was it against the law to have a drunk on the premises; he was beginning to offend the other patrons.

Ray finally decided that enough was enough and shut him off. He suggested that Mimi go home and sleep it off. Now Ray had a sense of humor but found nothing funny when Mimi responded that if Ray wouldn't serve him, then he'd come behind the bar and serve himself. He had been known to terrorize many bartenders.

Mimi was one of a clan of hard drinking, hard fighting brothers. He stood about six feet five inches tall and having worked all his life as a lumberjack was heavily slabbed with muscle. When he was drinking, he was not a man to tangle with.

Ray, at one hundred sixty-five pounds, was outweighed by a hundred pounds, and at five feet ten inches, he was shorter by nearly a foot.

Mimi's arms were immense and hung nearly to his knees. In a confrontation, anyone coming within range could be at a terrible disadvantage.

On this evening the bar was filled with young men and their girls, out for a few hours of enjoyment. The last thing that they wanted was a confrontation with Paul Bunyan. Spiritually they were in Ray's corner but practically speaking they stayed neutral and feared the outcome.

By this time Mimi had advanced menacingly around the corner of the bar and was closing the space that separated the two men. Ray didn't know the meaning of fear, and he could handle himself in a fight. He didn't want to see his barroom busted up along with his face. He suggested "If it's a fight you want Mimi, then let's take it outside where there's a little more room." Mimi turned and headed for the front door with Ray on his heels. Before he exited to the sidewalk where Mimi was standing with his fists raised, Ray turned to one of his patrons, Freddie Gautreau, and suggested, "If that son of a bitch cold cocks me, lock the door and call the cops. Drink all the beer you want until they get here."

Squared-off in the well-lit parking lot, the two circled one another, looking for an opening.

"Stop this bullshit and go to hell home, Mimi," advised Ray, but the advice only angered his opponent even more. He could see that their disagreement was not going to be quelled with words. Ray's thick forearm was able to deflect Mimi's opening jabs as each man searched for an opening.

With the length of Mimi's arms, Ray knew he could never score by standing toe to toe. Any advantage would have to be gained from fighting on the inside. If he could get in close enough without getting tagged, he might stand a chance. Being big with long arms was not necessarily an advantage when fighting a smaller, quicker man who understood the concepts and the physics of self-defense. Ray maneuvered to get inside the long reach of the belligerent man standing menacingly before him. Mimi could stand off all day and throw punches that in due course would churn Ray's face to a bloody pulp.

After taking a few jabs on his cheeks and forehead Ray saw his opening and moved in close. He knew he had to move fast. If Mimi wrapped those huge long arms around him, the little advantage he had would be gone.

Mimi's face and prominent chin were close and just above the top of Ray's head. If he was going to strike, now was the moment. He planted his feet firmly and drove an uppercut that grazed his own cheekbone on its way up. Ray's knuckles found their mark, dead on the point of the big man's chin.

Mimi's head snapped back with a paralyzing breakdown of all synaptic junctions. The rest of the massive frame followed the head, and he went over like a towering tree trunk. Unfortunately, the fight had strayed a bit close to the front of the building, and Mimi went back first, through the plate glass window onto the floor, back inside the taproom.

At that moment, a patron and his wife were on their way in. She let out a squeal as she exclaimed, "Oh my goodness, it's just like in the movies."

Freddy, the friend Ray had spoken to on the way out the door, fearing the worst had called the police. When they arrived a few minutes later they found Mimi still out cold on the floor, they called an ambulance. He woke up in the hospital, sore, but sober. When Ray refused to press charges, Mimi in grateful contrition came into the bar, apologized and insisted on paying for the glass.

Ray would talk about that fight from time to time; it had made him famous in the town. He wasn't a braggart, but news of the fight traveled fast. He didn't need to fight so often after that.

Most times, however, it was fun and foolish, and occasionally, overboard nuts. Take the night when a few of the boys, with a few too many under their collective belts, got into a loud, rollicking argument disputing the distance from the bar to the far end of main street and the post office. Around and around and louder with each pass the argument soon dwindled to "I'll betcha." Each participant adamant in their own point of view decided that to settle accounts an accurate measurement would be necessary. The only at hand instrument, for an accurate determination that the combatants could find was a yardstick. The end result… Three grown men on hands and knees at two in the morning worked their way down the sidewalk, counting out loud as the yardstick was rolled end over end for the entire mile. Occasional cars going by would slow, laugh with eventual understanding and drive on. Unable to rationally explain their antics to the local constabulary however, the three sobered up in the lockup.

Mill workers, salesman, and shopkeepers would stop at Ray's Lunch and get a beer. Some going to work, some coming home and some just passing through; the arguments were as loud as the laughter; the jokes and the language were all bad. But it was a great smelly bar. A local artist, for all the beer he could drink while doing so, painted larger-than-life wildlife scenes on the expansive walls creating an ambiance found nowhere else in town.

"If you will run the place for the two weeks I'll be gone, I'll get you a full-length beaver coat," he promised. "and I'll make some money as well."

"Well," Helen responded, "you'd want to go if fur wasn't paying a dime."

"No, I wouldn't," he responded. "It would have to pay, and I'm sure it will."

The whole endeavor would depend on her. She would need to do the banking, the ordering, tend bar in the evening, and in short, run the place. They both knew she could, it was just a matter of if, she would. She had the mouth and the disposition, both of which she could use to keep peace, order, and a sense of harmony in the raucous bar. It was a wearing place too; wearing on the nerves and on one's sense of harmony. But in spite of it all, and without the coat, she agreed to take charge of the bar for the two weeks that the men would need to take care of their business in the woods.

The two men understood the difficulty of getting into the backcountry and staying for a week at a time. Nine miles in from the top of East B hill and the nearest hard road was only one of the many obstacles they would face. Snow, feet deep, when added to the frigid subzero temperatures could make the expedition not only difficult but potentially dangerous.

Traps, about a hundred of them, would need to be hauled in and stored. Shelters would have to be built and stocked with food and other essentials like a stove, lanterns and fuel. Bunks would need to be built for sleeping.

Once the snows began to accumulate beginning in late November, easy access would no longer be an option. Any trip after that would be on foot and most likely on snowshoes. At these latitudes, in winter, and in the mountains, the sun arose late and set by 3:30 in the afternoon. On a hard, snow bound, trip like this, a man could leave before daylight on snowshoes, and not arrive until after dark.

During the late summer and early fall Ray and Henry made several trips back into "C" pond. The two men on scouting forays, would render notes on U.S. geological maps. This would enable the trappers to once again find the beaver colonies that could be buried deep under blankets of snow by trapping season. Two shelters were built about a mile apart. A sapling frame was sheathed in canvas and shrouded in tarpaper. Measuring approximately eight by eight by seven feet high, each would be heated with a small tin wood stove set just off the ground on flat stones... The stovepipe stuck out through the wall less than two feet above the ground. Bunks, one above the other, were matressed with a bale of hay and built diagonally across one corner. On top of the hay mattresses heavy sleeping bags would be rolled out.

"Not exactly the Ritz," Ray said, "but they'll do."

The traps were blackened by boiling them with bark to prevent rust and hung in trees adjacent to where they would be needed. Tin boxes used to prevent pilferage by the mice, were stocked with essentials like matches, whiskey, extra socks and toilet paper. The shelters were strategically placed about a mile apart to ensure the least amount of backtracking. They would optimize the limited time available.

Late fall hallmarked by deciduous vibrancy and the gentle smells of sweet decay also marked the last trip into the trapping grounds before the season opened on January first.

"Take that axe, Bill, and gather enough firewood. Stack it right there by the door. Get some birch bark too, for kindling."

Bill worked throughout the day dragging in fallen branches. Dry and well-seasoned the brittle wood easily chopped into stove length pieces. Hourly, the woodpile steadily rose.

It was a great time of year. The flies were gone, the temperature crisp and the bouquet of the air delicious A disarming reminder of the tempests to come.

As Bill went about his task of gathering and stacking the fuel pile, Henry and Ray put finishing touches on their shelters. The dirt floors were swept of pine straw. Sleeping bags were suspended from the ridgepole with wire in an effort to dissuade mice from nesting in the warm, down lining. A gallon of kerosene was squirreled away along with a lantern. Sugar, salt, coffee and oatmeal were added to the tin boxes. Bill dreamed, knowing it to be in vain, that he too would be here, like an early pioneer living in the wild and trapping for a living.

Upon completion, Henry looked into the interior and exclaimed, "It looks like a fire trap to me." With pots, pans, sleeping bags and a lone lantern suspended from the ceiling, straw on the bunks, pine needles and a stove on the floor, the interior had taken on the sloppy clanging appearance of an itinerant pot menders wagon from days long gone.

From the outside, the tiny tarpaper wrapped primitive huts each had a quaintness about them. Tucked into small brush choked grottos at the base of huge ancient spruce trees with massive overhanging branches, the structures were camouflaged into near invisibility. With the first snow it was suspected that they would disappear altogether.

"I hope they won't collapse from the weight of the snow," intonated Henry.

"Well," Ray said, as he dubiously looked the situation over, "if it doesn't burn down and it doesn't fall down, we should be okay."

A final check satisfied both men that nothing more could be done. Foodstuffs would have to be hauled in come January, on a toboggan, or in backpacks.

"You don't suppose anyone will bother this place, do you?" asked Bill, his face etched with concern.

"Hell, no," answered his father. "In a few weeks there'll be snow on the ground, and no one will be coming in here, and besides that," he continued, "they're not easy to see." To ease his mind once again, he said, "Naw, nobody will bother them."

The beautiful autumn days with their crispness and glory colors soon grew teeth. The crispness became biting and the cold masked the golden leaves beneath thick frost. Occasional snow flurries speckled the air and accumulated on the ground. The leafy branches were now stripped to bare boughs that clacked together in the freshening winds of on-rushing winter.

The men and the camps, such as they were, were ready. There were other things to keep him occupied. Bill had finally come to the realization that he could not be a part of this exciting expedition. But that was alright. There were other things to keep him occupied. In October, there was partridges. In November, there was the deer to go after, not that he had got one yet. Maybe this year. For the rest of the winter there was the rabbits. It had been a tough pill for him to swallow, but between school that was difficult for him, and his hunting he let the trip slip from his mind. It was not enough to concern him with what he would miss in January.

Chapter 2

THE INTERLUDE

A Shot gun replaces the fishing pole.

As far as Bill was concerned, Labor Day marked the end of summer. School was back in session, and the shotgun did replace his fishing pole. The green beneath Bill's feet began its metamorphosis to brown, as killing frosts repainted the landscape.

Little patches of snow would come and go as if Mother Nature couldn't make up her mind. The warmth of the days would battle the night's chill, in a war it couldn't win until spring.

Squirrels doubled their efforts packing nuts and seed into hidden niches, knowing it was their struggle that would sustain them through the blistering cold and deep snows of the approaching winter. In spite of the ominous signs of change this was the best time of year for Bill.

The season called for a boy, a dog and a shotgun, toss in a bit of gold and red leaf coloring, add perhaps a flake or two of snow and a sparkling Saturday mornings troposphere garnished with glittering frost and he had all the ingredients needed for a perfect day in the woods.

Partridges were non-migratory, commonly seen year around and hunted in the fall by the stalk and shoot method. He got the most satisfaction hunting the snowshoe rabbits with his dog Susie.

The migratory woodcock famously known as the timberdoodle followed a flight path down through western Maine during the snappy days of Fall. Susie was great for rabbit but useless for woodcock but that was okay. Bill was pitiful in his attempt to shoot a woodcock on the wing. His father was the expert.

Partridges would leave their night roosts for the early morning warmth of the sun splotched wood roads, and they made good targets for slow moving jeep riding hunters. The numbing cold slowed the birds' minds and stiffened their will to flee.

The Maine woods was home for the beautiful fan tailed partridges, and their meat was a welcome addition to any kitchen table.

"Take your time Bill," his father coached. "Go for the further first; you can get the closer one with your second shot."

The early suns warming rays had brought a pair of birds to the open woods road hoping to drive the overnight chill from their feathers and bones.

The two birds had wandered apart from each other, picking bits of gravel for their crops and insects for their bellies.

If Bill shot the closer bird one first, an easy shot, the second one was certain to escape. If he shot the further one first, he had a good chance depending on his skill to bag the both.

"You shoot too," implored his father. The uncertainty of his shooting skill evident in his voice.

"No. You can do this. You'll never know these things about yourself unless you try."

But Bill didn't trust his abilities: a bird in the hand is worth two in the bush. He shot the closer one first the other got away.

"What? His father grinned, "You didn't believe me?"

"That's not it" Bill protested. A look of disappointment and failure swept across his face. "I knew the minute that I shot, the closer one would fly, and I didn't think I was good enough or quick enough to get the other one."

Ray paused for a few seconds. He knew there was a lesson here for his son and he didn't want it to sound like a reprimand. "Son don't ever be afraid to fail, because if you are then you'll never win.

Just be certain that you don't gamble more than you can afford to lose. It's sort of like covering your bets."

Ray talked to his son often and when the opportunity was right, would spin an object lesson into the conversation. He wanted his son to do well in the world, and he hoped to assist in whatever small way he could.

Small game hunting in the fall, when the briskness of the frost covered mornings, evolved to afternoon warmth, when the early chill, thawed to a dampness that released the pungent aromas of leafy decay, gave Bill a feeling of oneness with the world around him. It was a partnership with his father, with his dog and with nature. Ray's dog Penney was a Brittany Spaniel whose skill at pointing out woodcock far exceeded Bill's skill at bringing them down. She had been acquired by his father when she was just a pup. She was the daughter of a field trail champion, her instincts were sound, and her early training had been effortless. Woodcock were her purpose in life. Working back and forth through the underbrush her sense of smell would draw her to quarry. The scent often just a few molecules floating on a whiff of air, would be enough for her sensitive nose. Suddenly her quick darting movements would cease as she came on point. One leg would be poised above the ground in mid stride, her bobbed tail unmoving, protruding straight back, and her vision riveted on her quarry. The small thick breasted bird would often set unmoving blending with the dead leaf ground cover, just a few feet beyond the tip of her nose.

When the bird broke cover it would ascend, nearly vertical until it cleared the top of the brush and then dart horizontally away from the hunter. The trick to hunting them successfully was the timing of the shot. There was a moment in time, that point of hesitation, when vertical flight became horizontal, when the shot could be made. It was a knack that Bill never quite mastered.

"I don't miss all the time," he defended himself, "just more than I should."

Woodcock hunting for him was always more frustrating than joyful. His father, on the other hand was skilled, a feat that he enjoyed not letting his son forget.

Susie, the beagle, wasn't at all like Penney, the Brittany Spaniel, Lady hunted by stealth. Penny hunted with endurance. Each season Susie, the intellectual beagle, with her superior gift of smell and endurance would really give the rabbits the run of their lives, literally.

The heavy evergreen covered ridges were replete with snowshoe rabbits, the next best thing to heaven for a boy and his dog. Susie was three years old, and she loved to drive rabbit as much as she loved her owner. During the week while Bill was at school and unable to take her hunting, she'd go alone, up on the ridge, behind Bill's grandfather's farm and drive rabbits, sometime all day long, with no one to shoot the game she chased. Her bay and drawn out yowls would echo along the ridges and down into the valley and some of the local farmers would look up from their work around the barns and regret that they had no time to be up there with that dog on her lonely chase. But, on weekends, Bill, up early to finish his chores, would grab his shotgun, "Come on girl, let's get a rabbit."

Each Saturday the neighbors would watch the boy and his dog walk the few miles out of town up beyond the town reservoir. For hours the two, working as a team, would get their limit. The little workhorse of a dog would pick up the fresh scent of a rabbit and trail it, yelping and yowling, her tongue lolling from her mouth. In great arching circles the two, dog and rabbit, would race through the snow-covered woods. The race didn't end until Bill, strategically placing himself, would shoot the rabbit.

Should he miss, Susie would stop and look at him as if to say," I did my job, I wish you would do yours" and then take up the chase once again. The team was inseparable in and out of the woods; the one seldom seen without the other.

Bill was a quiet kid preferring his own company, or his dogs, to that of others. It wasn't that he didn't like other kids, but he found, even at an early age, that his values were different. He liked to work, they didn't; he loved his father, they always seemed to be at odds with theirs; he loved the woods, where they liked the movies, hanging at the Pizza Shop and going to the Saturday night dances. He just couldn't find common ground on which to build a friendship. Above all, and it shamed him, they seemed to do so much better in school. He was in constant struggle for his grades. Being alone was easier. It was a shield against embarrassment; a protection from his shame. He understood that he wasn't as bright as the other kids in his class. By keeping to himself and keeping his mouth closed he knew he could get by. He knew he could get along.

In the late fall of November, the nature of hunting made a shift. Shotguns were cleaned, oiled and put away and the rifles were brought out. Hunting and shooting the small game of the woods was fun. The cold frosty mornings would give way to colorful sun warmed afternoons. The sounds and the quiet of the woods, were relaxing, but they lacked a certain quality that Bill couldn't quite define.

The hunting of deer however enveloped him into a cocoon of completeness and gave him a sense of adventure. It was like being invited to play in the majors after a lifetime in the minors.

Hunting only on Saturdays through the month of November just wasn't enough time. Bill always looked forward to Thanksgiving weekend. The long holiday weekend gave him Wednesday afternoon with schools' early dismissal, and Thursday morning before the big meal. All day Friday and Saturday he could be in the woods.

Wednesday's hunt came to an end without luck, as dusk settled in. Late November hunts were often helped with several inches of snow. The ground was soft, and the air was quiet. The dark silhouette of a deer stood out against the backdrop of white snow. This time of year, however, capricious weather could transform today's snowfall into tomorrow's rain. As Bill crawled from his bed this Thanksgiving morning, he could hear the soft rain patter on the porch roof outside his window. In the pitch, black of the early morning he made his way to the kitchen.

"Why didn't you wake me?" he asked as he rounded the doorway to where his father was making breakfast.

"I was just about to," replied his father as he poured the steaming hot coffee into the two waiting mugs. "You'd better sit and eat. It'll be light in an hour." Pausing long enough to pull his chair up to the kitchen table, "Where do you want to hunt?"

Bill, still a bit groggy, sat before his plate of eggs and home fries, "I don't know. How about up in back of Mitchell's sawdust pile?" It didn't matter that the sawmill hadn't run for more than twenty years and that the once great pile of yellow wood grindings had been reduced by time and insects to a slight raise in the landscape, now shot through with saplings.

"You know it's pouring out," the father offered as the son made the decision of where they would hunt.

"Yeah, but that's OK. We'll go in back of Mitchell's," a note of finality in his voice. "I like to hunt there."

Mitchell's Brook was made up as runoff from a chain of low ridges a few miles east of the county road that ran along the valley on its long trek to the Rangeley Lakes region. The brook splashed and pounded its way down from the ridges, ran behind the ancient sawdust pile, crossed under the highway and emptied into the Swift River. Ten miles downriver the flowage emptied into the Androscoggin on its long journey to the Atlantic. In the summer months, the brook was reduced to a dried-up bed of water worn granite boulders.

Deer hunting in the unbroken wilderness of Maine had a special flavor of its own. Maine hunting was not for the faint of heart.

"They've got a big pasture to run in," Ray was fond of saying, equating deer to cattle and the wilderness to a pasture. His theory was to cut that pasture down to size, by walking, covering some ground. Walking onto a deer or perhaps having one walk onto you was the best way to cut down on the size of their "pasture". "If it's too noisy to walk, then you of course, sit," he would instruct his son. The theory made sense to Bill and it influenced his hunting strategy.

In Maine, unlike other states where there were a lot of hunters Bill could walk a hundred miles each season and could count on one hand the men he had seen. Walking slow and quiet, dressed in "evergreen", men had walked within twenty feet of him and never knew; not until he cleared his throat or spoke, just to let them know of his presence. Episodes like that were rare. The vast expanse of forest precluded many such meetings.

Bill soon understood that when he walked in the woods, he needed a compass. A hundred yards into the woods, direction could lose its meaning. North quickly became confused with west, or east or even south. On one occasion without his compass, disorientation came so silently, so easily, so quickly, that he soon found himself back on the tote road that he had just left not twenty minutes before. Embarrassed and disconcerted he vowed never to leave home without his compass again. He not only always carried it; he learned the hard way to always believe it; even when he knew it to be wrong, but of course it never was. Walking while hunting as he nearly always did, he often would come out of the underbrush a mile or two from where he went in, but he always knew where he was in relation to the parked jeep.

From daylight until near dark, he would slowly, one careful step as a time, stopping often to watch and listen, close the distance on long looping jaunts. Regardless of the weather, he preferred to walk. Icy winds could be tossing frozen leaves on snowless bare ground, or gentle rains softening the ground under foot, he enjoyed being a part of the environment. A foot of wet snow would allow silent movement while at other times a blistering freeze would turn the ground to brittle crystals that shattered beneath each step. Fitting the noise, he made to the natural sounds around him challenged his abilities. The challenge was the joy. If he made noise, so would his quarry. Who would hear whom first?

Strain and exertion were a part of the game, sometimes the best part. He enjoyed the labor, and the toil, the demand, and the ordeal. This Thanksgiving morning, as in every other morning when Bill went hunting, this was his frame of mind.

Ray guided the jeep adjacent to the ancient now diminutive sawdust pile. Father and son sat and listened to the light rain splatter on the tin roof for a moment before discussing the direction that each intended to take.

"I would like to walk up along the brook until I get to the point on the side of the ridge where the brook begins to break up.

"From there," his father suggested to him, "if you swing off into a north-westerly direction, you'll get into a bunch of hog backs," his picturesque term for the undulating rise and fall of the land. Ray pulled on his cigarette in the predawn darkness as Bill watched the glow momentarily incandesce to a bright red.

"There's a lot of beech and oak trees up there. You just might catch a deer working the nuts." Bill had hunted in that area before and knew that eventually the topography flattened out and became boggy.

"Your mother has company coming for dinner today, so you plan on meeting me back here by two o'clock," and for emphasis Ray playfully grabbed his son at the back of his neck, "You hear me now?"

"Yes, Pop." To get back on track, Bill asked his father, "Where are you going to hunt?"

"I'll stay low at the foot of the ridge, working my way up and back. Not to be side tracked, his father once again repeated, "keep your eye on the time…. be back here by two o'clock."

"Ok pop, I will."

Exiting the jeep into the cold dampness, the two started out together, but soon diverged onto their separate paths. By ten a.m. Bill had come to the point where the main brook was no longer discernable. The rain continued unabated and the snow cover was beginning to melt away exposing the rotting vegetation beneath. Icy rainwater saturated his hat and ran alternately off the tip of the visor or down the back of his neck, depending on the tilt of his head. Wetness had finally saturated through his outer garments penetrating to his skin in places. Ripples of shiver ran up his spine as he hunched his shoulders, stretching his back muscles in a vain attempt to generate some muscle heat, to ward off the cold. The effect although feeling good was so momentary that within a few minutes the gesture needed repeating, endlessly.

Finally, after much exertion he was on top of the ridge where the ground stretched out flat before him. Wispy tendrils of fog floated among the wet blackened tree trunks and the spindly leaf stripped branches. Visibility was limited and without elevation the water lay in shallow snow caked pools that sucked his boots down into the mud and refused to relinquish them. The sun, low in the gray cloud choked sky, failed to cast a shadow. The patches of congealed white slush were all that differentiated the trees from the uneven ground. The mist accumulated in drops along the branches, and the only sounds in the featureless black and white din were their muffled splashes on to the sodden ground.

Replete with deer tracks the snow was pawed and churned where the whitetails had searched out nuts and other ground cover for graze. Their tracks were everywhere and reminded Bill of a well-trod sheep yard. He inched along, eyes and ears alert, searching for a movement or the sound that would give his quarry away.

With this much evidence of recent deer activity he hoped to at last get his deer. He was thirteen; soon to be fourteen and he hadn't as yet scored a kill. This was a point of deep embarrassment that he hoped to soon remedy. He considered himself a better woodsman and a better shot than many of his luckier acquaintances. His bad luck couldn't hold forever.

He would, every few steps, stand perfectly still for minutes at a time, straining his ears and constantly searching with his eyes. Acutely aware of anything that moved around him and chewing on triangular beech nuts, he would watch with detached interest the Chick-a-Dees that flitted from branch to branch within arm's length of where he stood.

For an hour he worked his way through the hardwood, frustration mingling with anticipation. He would soon need to turn and head back to the jeep and home. It wasn't easy to tell when he heard a sound in the woods. It was a place full of quiet sounds; a noise that didn't belong. "When you hear it, you'll know it." That's what his father had told him once.

He heard it and he knew it. It may have been a squirrel, or a bird even, but he knew it was something extra, an intrusive out of keynote, in the otherwise harmony of the woods.

With stealth that his father would be proud of, he ever so gently, quietly, levitated forward. And there it was again, the soft stirring of heavy wet leaves and snow. Visibility had improved. The great trees were further apart, and the underbrush was not nearly as thick. The misty low-lying clouds too, seemed to rise just enough. Experience was telling him that the sounds weren't human, but were they deer? With his heart beating like a base drum in his ears and in his chest, he had to stop, take a deep breath, and scold himself into relaxing. Sweat glistened on his forehead and his hands tremored from the adrenaline rush.

"Jesum crow, if I don't settle down, I might better throw rocks than shoot," he admonished himself.

Finally, he could see the movement that he had so vainly been searching. He knew the deer was right there in front of him, but he couldn't make it out. Not the head, not the shoulders. He couldn't go forward anymore; in fact, he couldn't move at all until he was ready to shoot.

"If I can see him move then he'll certainly see me." What to do thoughts raced in his mind as he inched his head from behind a tree to at last make out a great pile of antlers atop the biggest thick-necked buck he had ever seen.

The animal pawed gently through the dwindling snow, stopped, looked around, and then lowered his snout into the narrow ruts he had just made with his hoof.

Gently, Bill pulled back the hammer. Bill raised the 30-30 to his shoulder. At sixty yards it was a near shot and one that would shame him to miss. Fractions of a second before he pulled the trigger, the animal raised his head abruptly, pricked his ears forward, poised one hoof above the ground and looked directly at Bill. As the deer bunched his haunch muscles preparing to jump, the air split with the resounding crack of the rifle. He didn't know how much time would elapse from the time that the bullet left the barrel until it struck home, but it seemed like an eternity. The deer turned and jumped from sight. "I couldn't have missed him, I couldn't have," sprinted through his brain as he jacked a fresh cartridge into the chamber of his model 94 Winchester carbine, a gift from his father on his thirteenth birthday. Bill quietly raced to the spot where he had last seen the deer, grateful to find hair and blood. The dejection, of seconds ago, became elation. He had trained the open sights directly on the front shoulder, felt certain that his shot had been true, and hoped that the animal had not gone too far before the wound proved to be mortal.

Hit hard, high on the shoulder, the deer had raced across the flattened top of the ridge and down the backside. For the first fifty yards the buck's strides were long and fast moving, but even going downhill his effort of movement was becoming more difficult. He stopped to rest with increasing frequency and listened for anything in pursuit. The buck soon took to lying down often, and three hundred yards downhill from where he was hit the stag, no longer able to rise from his bed, died.

Bill, determined to not be denied his first deer had started out fast, disheartened by the length of his quarry's stride. The pursuit however soon slowed as the shortened steps and the increasing blood trail testified to the damage he had inflicted. Knowing that the buck would soon take to bedding down with increasing frequency, and in no hurry to force the deer to jump and run, he likewise slowed his pace.

After twenty minutes of careful tracking, he knew from the signs that he was getting close. Finally, ahead of him in the brush he saw the gray brown outline. Men had lost deer that suddenly sprang up and ran, never to be seen again. Not the case this time. As Bill drew close, he could see that the deer was unmoving and dead. Slowly releasing the hammer, for the final time he leaned the rifle and himself against the base of an old oak and took a deep breath. As with most things in his young life, he celebrated internally: alone. He was satisfied that he had accomplished something. It was a prideful moment for him.

Bill felt as good about things as he had ever felt in his young life. The shaking and the heart pounding were gone; he was warm, hot actually. He took off his hat and coat to prepare himself for the job ahead. The rain had dwindled to a gentle drizzle, but it was a relief to remove his heavy rain soaked outer garments. Entrails had to be removed, a job he had never done but had witnessed a number of times. Being so far back in rough terrain the lighter his burden the better. Even woods dressed the big buck was certain to weigh two hundred pounds. As messy and unpleasant as the job was, it was a precursor to the next job of dragging his prize out of the woods.

Before encircling the antlers with his pull rope, he checked the time. Coming up on two o'clock, Bill knew he'd catch hell when he got back to the jeep. Slumping his shoulders, taking in great gulp of cold air, casting his glance up the long ascent from which he had just came down; he began the incredible uphill drag. The carcass outweighed him by more than fifty pounds and the arduous task bordered on the impossible. Within minutes his shoulder joint felt unhinged. Changing his pulling arm gave him only scant minutes of respite. The number of steps between alternating arm changes steadily dwindled until he devised a scheme of fifteen steps… change arms… fifteen steps. The advance slowed still further as he added a brief pause with each change.

His lungs burned, his heart raced, and his arms and legs throbbed from the exertion. Level ground as he rounded the crest of the ridge, gave him a much-needed breather. The pull was increasingly becoming a race with the fast diminishing light. The dragging across the undulating ground of the hog backed ridge top was alternately cruel and compassionate. As the darkness began to overtake him the ground began to tip in his favor. Fatigue and darkness was taking its toll. His movements ns were becoming clumsy, and unseen twigs slapped his face. Fearful of losing an eye in the failing light, he finally admitted defeat and began to seriously think about what he must do. Leave the deer? Never! Keep going? Not practical! What then? Look for a spot to hole up for the night. Ten minutes later and within a few hundred feet of his decision, he spotted an old blow-down that in its fall had pulled up a large clot of dirt along with the exposed roots, leaving a shallow dirt roofed cave. He relinquished his hold on the pull rope and awkwardly backed his way into the muddy hole in an effort to escape the elements.

The heat of his exertions had generated perspiration that dampened his underclothes. At rest, the chill of the night air penetrated to his skin, and the blackness settled about him. One instance he could make out the silhouette of a nearby boulder, and an instant later he could see absolutely nothing. So black as to be tangible, the dark engulfed him. He couldn't, dared not, move for fear of injury. At first, he sat on his heels, but leg cramps forced him to sit on a cold, wet, slime-covered rock. Fighting the shivers and nodding off, only to wake, he suffered the misery of the damned. The fatigue, the cold, the wet; he resolved to accept it all for he had shot one hell of a deer and he meant to bring it home.

Between brief nodding off periods he made wagers with himself on how much trouble he'd be in, on gosh-darn Thanksgiving Day.

"Boy will she be mad," his mind kept repeating, picturing the red-faced anger he had seen before. The phrase rolled around on his mind's tongue, and dripped like an over ripe tomato, "Boy will she be mad."

Bill knew in his heart that his father would understand. "I'm sure he heard me shoot. If Dad heard, he'd figure out I couldn't get out before dark. He'll be waiting for me in the morning."

So sure, that his father would understand, he was able to ease his mind. For his father to convince his mother, would be a whole other can of worms.

"I'm sorry Dad," became his dominant thought as he sat hunched and quaking under the ball of roots and mud through the long, cold, miserable, wet, night.

Around three in the morning, the rain finally stopped. A slight wind began to stir its way through the trees gently shaking them. Huge droplets began to fall all through the dark unseen woods with resounding plops. Some hours later the light of dawn began to infuse the darkness. Bill, stupefied by the cold, bleary eyed and haggard, repeatedly stretched in a vain effort to generate a spark of body heat. Fingers and toes, cold to the point of brittleness sang with electric tingling as his movements reestablished the circulation. Glassy snot repeatedly was wiped onto the sopping sleeve of his wool jacket.

Surveying his surroundings in the awakening world he looked at the first nemesis of his young life and shook his fist: "I'll get you down off this darn mountain; I'll not leave you behind, even if it kills me." The buck was now stiff with rigor and doubly hard to drag. His unyielding limbs repeatedly tangled in the brush but going downhill was easier and within an hour he broke into the clearing near the ancient mound of rotting wood.

Bill knew without a doubt that his father would be waiting for him. He knew too that the first words from his father's mouth would be "Where in the hell have you been?" And that's exactly how it happened.

Years later Bill would look back and marvel that the best day of his life had been immediately followed by the worst night.

Arriving home, wet, cold and hungry, Bill immediately stripped himself of the sodden mud caked clothing and slipped into a tub of piping hot soapy water He soaked until the water began to cool and then went to his room for a nap. Looking back on his ordeal, it didn't seem so bad after all.

It was two in the afternoon when Bill, after working up his courage, decided to brave the kitchen. His mother wasn't speaking to him, but his father with a huge grin across his face took a different tact.

"Let me tell you about the time that your mother wanted to go jacking. It was before we were married, back when she was in nursing school at the Rumford Hospital".

"I don't think, you need to be telling him that kind of stuff," his mother scornfully interrupted.

Ignoring her as though she hadn't spoken, Ray continued with his story. "Ben, my brother and your aunt Celia were with us". Knowing that he was about to hear a good story, Bill pulled his chair closer to the kitchen table where he was comfortable and could rest his elbows on the Formica top. "I had a 1936 Dodge, so we cruised around in. We drank a little beer and waited for it to get dark. We finally decided to go over by East Andover where there were a lot of nice open fields. I always knew it was a mistake to go jacking from a car, but the women weren't dressed to be out traipsing around in the brush in the middle of a frosty cold night.

"So, what happened?" Bills' anticipation was getting ahead of the story.

"Well", continued his father, grinning in remembrance as he relived the events. "We drove down this old dirt road, flashing the light in the fields, when Ben spotted a set of eyes way the hell down at the far end of a field. Celia was driving, and she stopped the car. When we got out Ben passed me the rifle. "You're a better shot than me," he said. "And I was too!" It was black out that night and the only thing you could see was those two shinning eyes, nothing else. You couldn't see that deer's body at all. It was a long shot, and all I had for a gun was that Remington .30–open sight, no scope. I got down on one knee and had Ben stand with the light just over my shoulder behind me, so I could see my sights as well as those eyes."

Ray raised his empty hands, mimicking his actions and reliving those long-ago moments. "The second I pulled the trigger the eyes disappeared, and Ben doused the light. His voice rose a little in the telling. He too, Bill discovered, was getting caught up in his own story telling.

"I don't know what it was, but a glint or something, caught the corner of my eye. Several hundred yards up the road, where it came to a dead end, there were two wardens sitting in a car, just waiting for a couple of fools like us to come along. Anyway, I took off on a dead run down through the field in the direction that I had shot. Ben and the girls got back in the car, by the time he got it started, the wardens were right there. One of the wardens jumped out of the car and took off down through the field after me. It was pitch black and I couldn't see a thing, except the flashlight of this guy chasing me, a hundred yards behind me.

"Did you get caught?"

"If you wait a minute," his father ginned, "I'll tell you the rest of the story. I'm going to have a cup of tea. Do you want one?"

"Well no, I want you to finish the story." His father was a great storyteller and knew how to drag out the suspense.

"Anyway, I got a hundred and fifty feet into the woods and fell into a little brook that ran along the edge of the field, in a strip of woods. I just lay still; I didn't move a muscle. This warden finally comes to the edge of the drop off that leads down to the brook. He stood there, probably twenty feet from where I lay, but I didn't move. He stood there for a minute. I could hear him breathing. Pretty soon he swears, low sort of under his breath and turns back toward the cars. You can figure, he wasn't about to go chasing after somebody in the dark, in the woods. Not when the guy he's chasing has a rifle, and all he's got is a pistol and a flashlight. Good way to get himself killed."

"You wouldn't shoot him, would you dad."

"No, of course I wouldn't," but he didn't know that.

Ray paused to sip his tea and get a handful of ginger snaps.

"So, what happened next?"

"Let's see. Back at the car, the wardens search the car and the trunk, looking for a gun and a flashlight."

"Where's the gun?" he asks Ben.

"We ain't got no gun," he says.

"You just shot at a deer. We saw the light, and we heard you fire."

"No, you didn't, cause I didn't"

"The argument goes around and around, but there was no gun and no deer, so there was nothing that Ben or the girls could be charged with. The wardens had to let them go. I walked down the brook until I found an old hollow tree. I don't know how I found it, in the pitch black, but I did. I shoved the rifle up inside that tree as far as I could, then I followed the brook out to where it crossed under the road.

In the meantime, your mother drives down to the end of the dead–end road and turns around. The game wardens are right on her ass. At the end of the road the wardens pretend that they're going to park, but as your mother drives off, they follow with their lights off. Now I'm standing in the trees just off the road and I can see the whole thing, but I figure what the hell, even if they see me, there's nothing they can do. As the car slowly drives by, I jump on the running board, open the door, and as your mother slides over I get behind the wheel and keep on going. The wardens, driving behind us with their lights off, see this action. The headlights come on, the flashing blue and red lights come on and the siren comes on. They jump out of their car, and rush up to ours, demanding to see the gun. I tell them there is no gun that I was just in the woods taking a leak. They were madder than hornets, but without a gun, there was nothing they could do."

"So," Bill asked, "did you get your gun back?"

"Well, I didn't dare to go near the place for about two weeks, I knew that they'd be watching for me to come and get it. Finally, one morning, after deer season opened, I went up that old road parked my car, walked down into the woods and got the gun."

"Did you shoot that deer?"

"I walked over to where I thought I had shot, and he lay right there. It had to be one of the best shots I'd ever made, right smack between the eyes. And it had to have been over two hundred yards to the road. And another thing, talk about luck, when I ran down through that field in the pitch black, I just happened to run right through an opening in a barbed wire fence that went all the way around that field. If I had been ten feet to the right or the left, I would have got tangled up in it and got caught, sure as hell. So, you see," he concluded, glancing up at his wife, "we all make mistakes.

What was the mistake?" Bill asked, "going jacking or almost getting caught?"

With Helen looking on and within earshot, Ray didn't answer. He really didn't need to.

Chapter 3

BILL'S BIG BREAK

Thanksgiving was over and Bill's mother had finally gotten over the rage that had replaced the worry once she found that her son was alive and of one piece. Fear, that awful night, had kept her sleepless in spite of her husband's reassurances. How he could sleep in the face of such uncertainty worried her nearly as much as her son's absence. She lay in the dark that night, listening to the wetness outside, and pictured certain calamity. In the morning as the jeep pulled into the driveway, her son, cold, bleary eyed, and hungry stepped from the vehicle. The fear that she had harbored through the night mutated itself into a discordant rage; a rage that died a slow death. It took two days before the frost in her remarks thawed to a mother's warmth. Reprimands became admonishments which were replaced with cajoles never to do such a thing again.

The weeks that followed the seasonal unpredictability of fall finally settled into winter. Daily snow squalls added a few inches to the accumulating ground cover and cold blustery nights thickened the ice that covered the lakes and streams.

On Christmas Eve the wind that had howled for three days subsided and the first big storm of the winter season settled in. The brightly colored lights, subdued by the flake filled air and the blanket of fresh snow, gave a picture postcard quality to the empty streets and the frost glazed windows. As the New Year approached, the accumulation of snow along the roadside and in the fields loomed at two feet with more at higher elevations.

Bill never regarded Christmas as the grand and joyous event portrayed by the music, presents, and the gaiety; he simply viewed Christmas as another nice day. It was an extra day without school. He enjoyed the simplicity of the hymns but tended to ignore the spirituality. If there was a God, he'd rather hoped that he'd break Henry's leg so that he couldn't go trapping with his father. That would leave him. Bill understood that it wasn't possible for his father to go deep into the back country for a week without help.

With their upcoming trip less than a week away, Bill's father would clench his teeth in ill suppressed frustration. He watched, their chance for an easy walk, into "C" POND, fade. With the arrival of heavy snows so early in the season, neither Ray nor Henry harbored any illusions about the gut-wrenching difficulties that the trip had in store for them. Their backs, as well as their toboggan, would be loaded down with the necessities to sustain them for a week. The tempo in Bill's kitchen picked up in these last days of the old year. Meals were pre-cooked and packed. Three meals a day, for two men for a week, was a lot of food to be packed in jars or in tins and sat on the back porch to freeze. The shelves were loaded by weeks' end. On the morning of their departure a box of candy bars, a half-gallon of whiskey and a pistol was added to the load. They hoped to leave no essentials behind, or to add any extras. Pulling and carrying their necessities over, mountains and along the sides of steep wooded ridges, would tax the limits of their endurance.

The big day finally arrived, and the two men departed well before dawn on New Year's Day. Bill was outraged that he had slept thought their departure.

"Why didn't you wake me, for crying out loud," he wailed to his mother, genuinely angered that he wasn't there to see his father off. During the week of their absence, Bill daydreamed of their great adventure. With his father, in spirit, he endured and relished the hardships he was so certain that the two men were experiencing.

Gone for seven days the two trappers arrived back home late on a Sunday afternoon. Unshaven and reeking of stale body odor, wood smoke and tobacco, the two men laughed and talked of their experiences. Besides the two travel days they had sat their traps over a five-day period. In all a hundred and twenty traps had been set. Ice thicknesses had ranged to more than a foot, and with the heavy overlying snow, setting each trap had been an arduous task. From before daylight until dark they had worked at a fevered pace. They were out now and for the next six days would work their jobs and rest and prepare for a return trip to pull the traps and bring their catch to market. Two days later Ray got a phone call from Henry's wife:

"Are you OK?"

"Yah, fine. Why?"

"Henry's been sick ever since you got back, a lot of throwing up and a lot of pain in his belly."

"Maybe my cooking has something to do with it," Ray retorted with a grin but without humor. They had a lot of traps under the ice, a long way in the back country, and without Henry, he wasn't sure what he was going to do.

Two days later Henry was in the hospital suffering from a gallbladder attack precipitated apparently by stones the size of golf balls. Henry's return trip to the woods was out of the question. Bill was quietly overjoyed even as he mouthed empty platitudes of sympathy for his father's trapping partner. "What are you going to do Dad?" Bill was not a believer in prayer, but this turn of events gave him pause for wonder.

"Gee.... that's a shame." Bill saw it as his chance of a lifetime. An opportunity like this would not come again and he meant to press his advantage.

Maine State trapping laws were restrictive and demanding and in Bill's estimation not all together fair. They were guidelines, however, that he had to observe at the risk of breaking the law. No one could help another trapper unless he too had a license. Translated, it meant Bill couldn't cut a hole in the ice, or get a pole ready for a pole set, or carry the ice chisel, or even carry his father's pack basket for that matter. The risks of getting caught, however, were slight. The game warden had to observe the infraction with his own eyes and where they were going, the chances of that were slim. If the wardens showed up back in that country, I'll tell them I'm just the cook, he thought grinning at the prospect. Through the years Bill had helped his father often. He had cut holes, gathered bait, prepared the traps, removed beaver from sets, and even carried the rolled-up hides back to the jeep, all without being seen.

He was well schooled in the art of trapping and he had been a great help to his father. The one thing he was not yet capable of doing and wasn't trusted to do was to skin out a carcass, when a slight cut through a hide could translate into dollars lost. But he knew that his other abilities would more than compensate for this one deficiency.

As a young boy, he liked trapping because his father liked it so much. With a wish to emulate his father, he would drag himself from a warm winter's bed when to stay behind was easier. Never told, "You're going," just asked, "would you like to go?" He was always there and ready. To help matters along his father always took the time to explain what he was looking at and how he might translate what he saw. Animal signs, when thought through could be read like a book.

All the animals of the woods were survivors. They lived hard lives and often skirted their own death with stealth, speed, strength, and awareness. All wild animals had their own kind of habits, and cautionary ways to keep them alive, safe and fed. Ray spent hours teaching his son the things he had learned. As the teaching brought them closer, Bill found that he too loved the challenge. As a boy Ray, had trapped for money, Bill did it for a whole different reason.

Trapping was hard demanding work and not for the faint of heart. There were still hidden corners of Maine relatively unchartered and perhaps, Bill liked to believe, had never been trod upon by a white man's foot. It was to these places that beaver would migrate. Remote secluded valleys and concealed mountain top meadows.

Once winters icy covering formed, the beaver were locked into a cold, dark underwater world. Their only respite was the black unseeable world within their domed lightless nest, beneath feet of mud and sticks and hard packed snows. A tunnel leading from their dry nest down into the water world beneath the ice was used to retrieve bark-covered branches. As the only source of food for a long desolate winter the wood pile outside the tunnel entrance was often immense. It was into this hard-cold forbidding world that the trapper needed to trek his way. Ice, often sixteen inches thick had to be chiseled through in zero-degree temperatures. The trap set on a platform on a pole would be lowered through a hole in the ice while the wind would be gusting from ten to twenty miles an hour. Bill, ever wanting to please his father, and more, wanting to be like him, taxed and stretched himself in a never-ending quest to achieve that goal. In time his father's domain might become his own. The woods, outdoors, the openness, were loved for their own sake and not just too gladden his father.

In hunting as well as trapping, he loved the challenge of endurance; the cold, the climb, the distance, and finally the kill. These things hardened him and helped him to comprehend a kind of single-mindedness in purpose. He supposed that hardships, self-imposed or not forced him to come to terms with himself; to understand his abilities, his shortcomings and how to overcome them. Spending that night in the woods only a few months earlier, alone and unafraid, cold and wet, with no place to seek comfort had been one of those times. It was one of the many lessons he would endure on his personal road to manhood. This trapping experience with his father, his hero would be another. Henry's misfortune would be his good fortune and school or no school; he was bent on going. His father couldn't go it alone and the trip had to be taken. With thousands of dollars' worth of fur in those traps it would be criminally irresponsible not to get them out. Bill did not believe in fate, but fate had dealt him a hand and he meant to play it.

"Please Pop; you've got to let me go."

"No," there was finality in his father's voice that Bill simply chose to ignore.

"You're too young and you've got school."

Bill heard his father, but Ray had cast a look from the corner of his eye to his wife; a look that Bill saw and interpreted as crumbling resolve.

"I'll make up the work. I'll do it before we go. I'll do anything" The barrage of what he would do tripped from his mouth as fast as he could form the words.

"A learning experience, that's what it is. You want me to learn, don't you?" Becoming more animated with each rushing word, he fell to his knees in beseachment.

"I don't think so," responded his mother with the faintest touch of doubt, "you don't do all that well in school now. How would it be, you missing a week?"

"I'm not giving up on this," Bill adamantly replied, "besides Pop you're going to need me. Suppose you catch a hundred beaver. You can't bring them out alone. Heck, the skins would weigh three hundred pounds." "What if you break a leg? Who'd go for help?" Piling one bad scenario upon another, "it's dangerous and you know it, think about it." with his voice rising an octave or two.

"Heck, I might end up saving your life…. You never know." A smile of logic and possible victory played across his animated features. With a swaggering bravado, he knew he had not yet earned "you know that I'll be going, so you might as well give in right now." Bill and his parents exchanged meaningful looks and the room fell silent.

Somewhere along the course of working together the relationship had transcended the closeness of father and son. It enjoyed the intimacy of equals. Ray understood and silently approved. He wanted his son by his side. Bill knew that he had much to learn and knew too that his father would teach him. He was a willing student who also knew that he had things to offer.

"Pop," he repeated. "I've got to go." A subtle plea had entered his voice, "I'll be an asset, not a burden."

"I know that," his father responded. "I'm just worried about your schooling."

"I know I'm not a good student, but I'll make up the work, I won't fall behind."

"I'll talk to your mother," nodded his father as he more or less conceded to his sons beseeching eloquence. Later that night in the big feather bed Helen pulled over close to her husband of more than twenty years and quietly voiced her fears for him to consider. After some minutes of frustrated argument against the idea, she asked, "What are you going to do?"

"I guess I'm going to take him."

Deep vibrations from their voices could be heard throughout the house. Bill in his downstairs bedroom couldn't hear the words but knew his future was being decided on the floor above.

"Jesus Ray, he's only thirteen," Helen insisted.

"I know how old he is, but he's big for his age; I don't just mean in his body, but in his mind too. I think he's strong enough to do the job. Except for the walking in…. or for that matter, the walk out," Ray continued, "I don't have many doubts." Lying in the dark, listening to the alarm clock tick, he finally spoke the last he would say on the subject. "Christ, the walk almost killed me, and it didn't do Henry any good either.

Chapter 4

INTO THE BREACH

Snow encrusted, dirty from salt and sand with icicles hanging raggedly from the wheel wells, the jeep sat lifeless in the driveway. It was fully packed with a week's supply of frozen grub. The night before, Bill had retired early in anticipation of a quick start. For the past few days, since his father's reluctant surrender, he had dreamt and talked of little else. Sleep didn't come easily as his brain raced. Finally, late in the night he drifted off only to abruptly come to full wakefulness with a single rough shake from his father.

"You going with me?" he asked rhetorically.

"What time is it?" Bill queried as his bare feet hit the cold wooden floor.

They spoke in hushed tones out of respect for the early hour.

"Five o'clock", came his father's terse reply as he watched his boy rub crusty granules from his eyes. "It's about ten degrees outside, so dress right"

A few minutes later as Bill made his way to the kitchen, he could hear his mother and father conversing over their coffee.

"Yes," they had everything and "yes" they'll be careful, and "no" he wouldn't let anything happen to her "baby" boy.

Breakfast was soon over, and final goodbyes were exchanged as the two headed for the door. There had always been sharpness between his parents; a thin wedge of indefinable discord; an undercurrent of disapproval. It had, as near as Bill could discern, always been there. It was different from other marriages, civil for the most part, but certainly different. So, he felt a twinge of gladness as he watched his father and mother kiss their goodbyes to one another.

The hard-vitreous snow crunched beneath felt lined rubber packs as they made their way to the jeep sitting frost encrusted in the predawn moonscape. Everything creaked, the hinges that resisted the doors movement, the springs beneath that accepted the weight, the icy vinyl covered seats so cold and slippery to the touch. Even the engine, with its crank case of oil now turned to semi-congealed ooze, creaked as it slowly turned and jumped to sputtering life on the first try.

For ten minutes the engine slowly warmed and tendrils of heat rose through the ductwork and defrosted the windshield. The vehicle finally began to move down the drive and onto the main road on its frozen rubber tires. As the tires warmed to roundness the ride became less bumpy. The man and his son headed north and out of the still sleeping town. The snowbanks along the roadside were more than three feet high, a bit unusual for this early in the season, a sure sign they would be mountainous before spring. The headlights reflected off the snowbanks and produced a bright eerie tunnel-like-halo that continually advanced ahead.

At this early hour, they met few cars along their route. Occasionally a light from behind frosted kitchen windows in the hamlet of Andover testified that morning was not far off. A few miles beyond the small town brought them to the end of the plowed road. From this point on the gravel road was not maintained in the winter months. There were no houses between here and Errol, New Hampshire, a distance of some twenty-five miles so there was no need to plow.

In the early light, Ray stopped where the unplowed road began and lashed chains onto all four tires. With the jeep in four-wheel drive it became a formidable snow traveling machine. For several miles they churned along the snow-covered lane to the rhythmic clanking of the chains slapping against the fenders. They arrived at the top of East "B" Hill where Ray turned the jeep around facing toward home and parked in the middle of the desolate old snow bound byway.

"There'll be no one through here till spring" he explained to his son. "Besides, we may need a downhill running start when we're ready to get out of here."

As Bill opened the Jeep door the chilled night air assaulted his face with a ruthless hardness. He ignored the cold and silently let his boots sink into the eighteen Inches of unending whiteness.

The food they would need for a week was loaded onto the toboggan and packed into their back packs for the trip.

As early morning sunrays were breaking over the east ridge the two strapped on their snowshoes and backpacks and eyed the spot where they would leave civilization for a week. A week that promised unforgettable moments of hardship, humor, endurance and friendship; encouragement and discovery. Sixty years later, the events that unfolded during this upcoming week remained fresh and vital in Bill's nostalgic recall.

"Are we all set?" Ray asked as he adjusted the straps of his backpack and reaffirmed his grip on the toboggan pull straps.

"I think so," Bill replied and under his breath continued, "I hope so".

Ray said nothing but grinned in response. He tapped the live ash from his pipe and put it away. He adjusted his wool cap low over his scarlet topped ears.

"Then let's get going." He plunged down off the roadway onto a steep decline that soon leveled out to the long undulating trek, Ray led the way.

It hadn't snowed any significant amount in the week since Ray and Henry were here last; the trail was open, well packed and relatively easy to traverse. "Even when it's easy; it's hard," Ray joked to his gasping son on one of their rest stops. Midmorning brought with it a modest rise in the temperature. "A real heat wave," Bill suggested as he oriented his face to the sun's rays hoping to catch a little warmth on his cold inflamed cheeks.

Springs, percolating cold crystal-clear water to the surface from deep underground, were abundant along the trail. Once the water emerged from its deep underground protection it sheeted on the snow forming a blue white frozen cascade, ribbed and knobbed by the rocks and roots beneath. Its contours and delicate colors changed daily with its ever-flowing water, fluctuating temperatures, and new falling snow. To ward off any hint of dehydration, they would stretch full length on the ground and drink heavily and often. Sometimes completely camouflaged, the water's presence was only detectable by the telltale trickling sound from deep beneath the snow. Acting as a thermal blanket the snow kept the springs from freezing. Their origins were easily found when Bill would poke around in the snow. The hollow domed snow roof would collapse, exposing the pool of water beneath.

"Why doesn't it freeze, Pop."

"That water is coming straight up from deep below the frost line. Its warmer and under pressure; hard to freeze, unless it gets a lot colder than it is now."

Not sure he was completely satisfied with the answer, Bill in his exhausted state, accepted the explanation without an argument.

By one o'clock they both were feeling the effects of the constant exertion, but Bill was beginning to toil. The last thing he wanted was to have his father see him struggle, but in spite of his efforts, he lagged behind. For minutes at a time his father would disappear from sight.

On one occasion, his father well rested, sat on a stump smoking his pipe as Bill, panting and laboring with fatigue, pulled abreast. "Well I'm rested," he chided his sagging son, "time to get moving again".

"Just wait a minute will you," exasperation rather than humor edging Bill's voice in spite of his father's obvious enjoyment at his son's expense. Finally, the ground leveled off to a forest of mixed growth. Pine and spruce mixed with hardwoods offered open panoramic views unobstructed by new growth and underbrush. The flat terrain made for easier going and the two finally got some rest while walking along at an easy pace.

By 2:30 the sun was low in the sky; shadows were becoming long. The first of the two camps were close. When it finally came into view Bill could hardly recognize it as the same one, he had helped build the previous fall. Tucked well into a thicket of evergreen the black tar papered structure was hardly visible despite the white backdrop. Icicles draped in sheets from where the walls angled over to become the roof, and the roof was hiding beneath a thick blanket of snow. Branches, from the surrounding trees, were bent by their clinging burden of snow onto and around the tiny hut.

Ray and Henry had occupied this shanty for a week, ending just a week ago. The pile of firewood partially covered now lay in the open where Bill had stacked it months earlier. Bill shed his snowshoes and pulled on the door. It opened grudgingly sweeping a path through the recent snows. He howled in amusement as he peered into the dark windowless interior. Hanging from the ceiling were icy stalactites; the result of condensation and a leaky roof. The floor was frozen slick with icy knobs arising where droplets of water from the ceiling had fallen and froze.

Camp was made right by knocking the icy spears from the ceiling and sprinkling ashes, from the cold wood stove, onto the floor. A fire was rekindled in the tin contraption passing for a stove. The two busied themselves with unpacking and organizing what they had brought in with them. Bill bombarded his father with a constant reign of questions, which in turn Ray did his best to answer.

"Where's the first colony of beaver?"

"Will we be sleeping here tomorrow night"?

"What's for supper?"

"How thick is the ice?"

"Do you think we'll catch a lot of beaver?"

"Am I sleeping on the top or the bottom bunk?"

"Will you stop talking for a few minutes and fill this bucket with snow. We're going to need water for supper. And don't use any yellow snow," he added as Bill grabbed the bucket and slipped out the door. He stared into the darkness, unmoving. The rich array of stars and the sliver of light from around the door was all that kept the blackness at bay. The moon had not yet risen. The eeriness of the night was accentuated by the quiet whisper of air resonating through the pines. Everything around him was brittle with coldness, and as he scooped his kettle through the snow, he heard a distant muffled tearing. Later over supper Ray explained that a tree could freeze to its core and when it did, expand and rupture the bark. "Just like a bottle of milk that bursts when it freezes, and that's probably the sound you heard."

At these northern latitudes, the winter sun set early. Throughout the mid-day the temperatures had hovered comfortably in the twenties. The loss of daylight hammered the thermometer. The drop-in temperature was tangible and penetrating. It pressed in on the flimsy camp like a vice, a tiny bubble of heat in a vast ocean of cold.

A block of frozen spaghetti sauce was coming to a boil on the stove. The tang of burnt bread and sauce filled the narrow space as Ray sipped on a tin cup of appetite stimulating…whiskey and water. Bill didn't need anything to whet his appetite. As the plates of food became ready, they sat side by side on the edge of the lower bunk, ducking their heads to keep them from striking the upper braces.

The gloomy overcrowded interior, a jumble of discarded clothing, backpacks, boots and more, was becoming oppressive from the heat. The kerosene lamp cast long smoky shadows and in spite of the plummeting outside temperature the rising heat began to melt the ceilings layer of frost. Large accumulating droplets with increasing frequency began to plop onto their heads and into their plates. What started as a smiling tolerance of the situation soon degenerated to a hysterical side aching episode of unrestrained laughter. Wherever the indoor "rain" storm wet the floor a thin shiny layer of ice began to form. They quickly found that the best way to combat the treacherous condition was to sprinkle dead ash from the stove onto the floor. By weeks end the dirtiness and oozy black mud threatened to become a health hazard. The poor lighting prompted casual discussions of premature blindness, and there was a constant concern of catching colds brought on by the wildly fluctuating temperatures both in and out of the hut.

As the stove cooled following supper, and the hot flames subsided to a bed of glowing embers, the blistering outdoor chill penetrated the thin walls and raised fine lacey crystalline hoarfrost that sparkled in the subdued lighting. Once again, the stove would be stoked, the temperature would rise, the walls and ceiling would melt, and the men inside would become bathed in their own sweat.

"Are you hot?"

"Roasting"

"Me too" replied the older man as he removed his outer shirt in preparation for bed.

"I'm scared of that tin stove," Bill related to his father at one point, as the thing snapped and popped. The metal would turn cherry red in the dingy light as it twisted and contorted from the heat within.

"You take the top bunk," Ray suggested. "I sometimes have to get up in the night."

"Be sure to wear your boots if you do," laughed Bill as he did a paddy whack with his boots on the sloppy muddy floor.

Peeling off boots, pants, and more shirts down to their long johns, they crawled into their respective sleeping bags. Their long underwear wouldn't come off for a week. Exhausted by the long hard day and exhilarated by thoughts of the days to come, Bill lay quietly sleepless in the dark.

"We could both die if the canvas should catch on fire, couldn't we?"

"Yeah, we could," responded his father," that's why I just went out and wet the wall where the stove pipe goes out through." After a brief pause, "you should keep an eye on it too. "What did you wet it with," Bill asked, half grinning in the dark? "Have people died doing this kind of thing?" he asked not waiting for an answer.

"Well not quite like this, I hope." Ray laughed and then added on a serious note, "If anything should happen to me, you're only a hard day's walk out of here, you know. Now up in Alaska, trappers have died in the woods, after a fire or an injury. They were too far back in the woods to get out. I have read a number of stories of men who ate their dead partners, just so they could stay alive until spring."

"Don't worry Pop, you're safe. You'd be too tough to eat anyway… can you imagine?" Bill continued thoughtfully, "eating a man, God!"

His father laughed and then lying in the dark related the story of the trapper, who in a hurry to check his traps cut a small hole through the ice, big enough to reach down with his arm to feel if anything was in his trap. In doing so he tripped the jaws and caught his own fingers. Unable to pull himself free and in eminent danger of freezing to death out on the ice, he had reached down with a knife in his other hand and cut his fingers off to free himself.

"Could you do something like that, cut your own fingers off, I mean?"

"In the first place, I hope I never get stupid enough to check a trap that way, but when the alternative is dying, it's not a hard decision to make. The hard part," he chuckled, "would be to make sure you didn't drop the knife."

"Do you believe in luck Pop?" He asked his father as he scratched his initials in the thick hard frost gathered on the walls beside his bunk. As exhausting as the day had been, he was not yet ready to surrender to the fatigue that was relentlessly engulfing him. Faint ghostly images, made just visible by the thin ribbon of yellow glow escaping from around the ill-fitting stove door, captured and held his attention.

"No, I don't believe in luck," came his father's quiet reply, "but I do believe in opportunity."

"What's the difference?" Bill softly asked, getting closer to his moment of oblivion.

"I think luck is too arbitrary," came a response from the bunk below him. "What I do believe in is opportunity. Opportunity is around us all the time; it's everywhere, and I think that all it takes is a little vision, a little courage, and usually a lot of hard work. You mix them all together and you know what you get?"

"Luck?"

"Luck!"

"Now, get some sleep will you, and we'll see how lucky we are in the morning."

Chapter 5

NIGHT TALKS

The night had been a horror. The law of nature predicting that heat would rise proved to be as unexpected, and as unforeseen, as it was true. Lying in his top bunk just below the frosty ceiling, Bill fell off into a deep muscle rejuvenating sleep only to be dragged up to consciousness two hours later. He was bathed in a mixture of sweat and drippings from the now defrosted ceiling. It didn't take long for the tiny stove to heat the narrow space between the top bunk and the roof.

The bunks had been built in one corner, bridging the back and the sidewall. The bunk Bill slept on was a foot shorter than he was tall and prevented him from stretching out flat. His only recourse was to lie on his side in a semi-fetal position with his butt tucked back into the corner. Any change in his position would only result in a yet more uncomfortable one and in addition would cause hay chaff to rain down onto his father sleeping in the bunk directly below.

Bill found that without a window to open, the only respite from the heat was to set the door ajar just a crack. With the door open, the accumulated heat tumbled out, and cold air rushed in, leaving a frost trail along the floor. The temperature dropped in the room as the fire died in the stove and Bill fell back into a dreamless sleep. Before too long however, the frigid air suspended near the floor and the lower bunk brought his father out of a timber rattling snore, shivering from the cold. He arose, silently cursed his son, and closed the door against the onslaught of inrushing cold. He once again stoked the fire and retreated to his bunk and sleep.

The cycle once established took on a life of its own and repeated itself every few hours until morning's faint streaks brought it all to a bleary-eyed halt.

Breakfast consisted of a belly full of oatmeal loaded with brown sugar and rethawed canned milk. Hot tea had enhanced the flavor of burnt toast scorched directly on the smooth top of the hot tin stove.

Sipping the last of his tea, Ray mulled the day's upcoming labors. Consulting his hand drawn map, and his memories of a week ago, he pointed out the route they would take.

The plan was to strike along the east side of the valley, pulling traps as they went. The used traps would be hung in trees to be retrieved in the spring. Moving at a steady pace it would be late in the day before they got to camp two. It would take another day to clear the traps in the area. "So, we'll spend two nights over there," he told his son, "before we head back here." Bill slipped out the door, breakfast dishes in tow. In the biting morning chill, adhering food bits froze instantly and easily flaked from the tin plates. When they returned to this camp in two days' time, he planned to give them a good soap and hot water scrub.

Arriving late on the previous afternoon and being exhausted he hadn't stopped to take in his surroundings. Now, the tranquility of the moment gave him pause.

There is an austere serenity that encompasses the remote Maine backcountry when layered in snow and brittle cold. Bill stood quietly outside the flimsy half-closed door in the freshening morning light. Unflinching in the penetrating bitter chill, he marveled at the pristine noiseless beauty around him. The crystal blue flawlessly clear sky tinged with pre-sunrise pink in the east, accentuated the reverence he felt for the place. It was like being alone in a grand and empty church," he thought.

The temperature gauge nailed to the tree in front of the shack hovered about the zero mark, but with no wind and clear skies, the day was destined to be a good one.

"Come on, get those dishes cleaned up, we've got to get going." Jarred from a momentary detachment by his father's command, Bill bent to the task of cleaning the breakfast dishes. Using snow and his mitted hand he scrapped the crumbs from the plates.

"What will you want me to do?" Bill asked as he reentered the door and watched his father ponder the map.

"Your job will be simple," he said looking at his son. "Pull that toboggan, and chop holes in the ice." The grin on his father's face suggested levity, but he knew his day would be a hard one.

The first shafts of morning sun pierced the dense greenery at their acute angle. Reflections from the crystallized white ground cover caused the trappers to squint as they climbed into their snowshoes and made ready to leave.

"Let's go!"

They traveled light, pulling the toboggan lightly packed with the tools of their trade and two days provisions for their stay at camp number two.

The bone tearing monotony of the strength sapping work kept talk to a minimum. Bill was familiar with the work to be done. Penetration of the numbing cold through the layers of wool clothing was kept at bay by the exertions of their labor. Referring occasionally to his hand drawn map the two moved from one beaver colony to the next leaving scarlet hideless carcasses in their wake.

As Bill pulled the drowned animals up through the icy holes and their watery graves, he felt no remorse or shame. He was free of empathy and simply regarded the catch as a bit of cash for the family pocket.

That night lying in their bunks, at camp number two, an almost exact replica of the first camp, Bill wondered at his lack of concern and asked, "Does it bother you Pop, to kill those animals so some society woman can wear a fur coat?"

"No, not much. I'm just a guy at the bottom of the financial heap trying to make a living the best way I can. Hell, a whole industry depends on guys like me. The buyers, the tanners, the trimmers, the tailors and finally the guys that own the stores that sell the coats."

"It seems like an awful waste. Are beaver good to eat?" Bill asked, once his father paused. Ray then continued, picking up the thread of his answer, before Bill had gone off on his little tangent.

"I kill a cow for my steak and for my shoes and I kill a pig for my bacon, why not a beaver for my coat."

"You're getting a little poetic aren't you Pop?" came Bill's rejoinder while pondering his father's logic.

Continuing as though his son had never spoken, with a touch of sadness in his rhetoric: "there will come a day, ya know, maybe within your lifetime when there will be no more wild things."

"What in the heck are you talking about, Pop?"

It took a few minutes for a reply. Lying in the near dark with only a thin ribbon of yellow from around the stove door to light the room, the answer finally came.

"They'll all be kept, if they are kept alive, in parks or ranges or zoos. The woods will be sterile. If the hunters and the trappers don't kill them off, then the press of humanity will.

"You think.... You think there will be houses in here," the crack of incredulity, touched with a hint of mockery in his son's voice.

Brought back from his nostalgic foray into the future, "You laugh if you want, but when I look at the changes in my lifetime, I have no doubt. I just hope I don't live to see it." Moments of silence slipped by punctuated with only the snap of burning wood and the occasional creak of the frozen canvas walls.

"When a beaver dams a brook and water floods across a road it won't be tolerated. Their dams will be blown, and they won't survive. It'll happen slowly but someday they'll all be gone. It's going on all the time, all around you, in Africa, everywhere: lions, elephants, and the gorilla. To a zoo or dead, but they're all going."

He stopped occasionally and pulled on his pipe, its aroma filled the shack, and tendrils of smoke could be seen as they crossed the thin curtain of light streaming from the stove!

"Only the government has the power to stop such a thing.

To change the subject, have you thought about your future at all?" Ray inquired.

"No", Bill replied, rolling onto his side looking for a comfortable spot. "I'm having enough trouble getting through school."

"That's okay" his father mused. "Don't strike off into any direction too soon. Don't box yourself into anything. And don't worry about your grades just yet. Just keep on plugging, don't get discouraged, and don't give up. There's something else I think you should remember."

"What's that, Pop?"

"Don't take the easy way. Somewhere down the road, in your future, you're going to have decisions to make."

"Like what?"

"Like…are you going to take this good job, or are you going to go to college for the next four years?"

"And?" Bill asked.

"And," his father said finishing the thought, "you might make the harder choice and go to college. When it's all said and done, the education will probably last a lot longer than the job."

Before Bill finally sank into sleepy oblivion, he heard the last of his father's ruminations. "Remember, if it's ```easy, everybody will be doing it, so don't take the easy way."

And then it was quiet as Ray, the philosopher, and his son slept. Groggy semi-consciousness was brought on with the nighttime ritual of temperature gymnastics and the restlessness of a mouse in Bill's bunk hay.

The new day brought few surprises, but the monotony of the work was interrupted when they trekked through a swampy growth of cedar and came upon a "deer yard". Several deer were spotted attempting to elude detection in the thick undergrowth and deep snow.

"Look pop, they're everywhere," Bill spoke in undertones, not wishing to disturb the deer.

"We're in a deer yard," he told his son in a subdued voice.

"What's a deer yard?"

"Well," he said, "As the snows get deeper through the winter months, the deer congregate in places like this, where there's cedar or hemlock to feed on. They keep paths beat down and they stay right here until spring. If they get off the paths, with their spindly legs they sink up to their bellies, and there stuck."

"I've heard of places up in Canada where a pack of coyotes get into a yard and kill them all."

"That's awful," Bill, thought, as they veered away from the "yard" and back toward the next colony of beaver.

The work was as unrelenting as the temperature throughout the morning hours. The catch was plentiful as they pulled in many large blanket beavers that would fetch handsome prices when stretched and dried. As the afternoon wore on the pleasantness of the day began to abate.

The temperature that until around two o'clock had hovered in the upper twenties now began to drop.

"It's getting colder. Can you feel it?"

"Yah Pop I can. It's going to be a bugger tonight."

Tired and hungry they arrived back at the camp around 4:00 o'clock. Their supper had set on the stove since that morning and had long since gone cold. The evening meal of sliced roast beef, small potatoes and peas, all immersed in thick brown gravy was soon brought to a boil above the newly kindled fire. Helen had prepared and froze in quart-sized containers the meals that her husband and son now heaped praises on.

Bill got his first taste of whiskey that evening. A shot mixed with a spoonful of honey and a cup of boiling water. The concoction drove the chill from him and fostered a ravenous appetite. Evening became night and the two retired to their bunks, still clothed in long johns and socks.

Bill enjoyed the interlude between bedtime and sleep, picking his father's brain endlessly.

"Pop, are we rich?"

"Are we rich! Hell no, we're not rich."

"We're not poor?"

"No, we're not poor either, just comfortable. As long as your mother and I stay healthy, and the bar keeps doing well, then we'll be all right."

Bill wasn't sure he fully understood the concepts of rich and poor. He had a roof over his head and there was always food on the table. He understood rich only in its relationship to work. The harder a man worked, the more money he made, so if you work really hard you could get rich. Then his father put a twist In Bill's logic.

"Hell, if I was rich, I wouldn't work so hard."

"Are all black men poor?" Bill asked." Have you ever met a black man?"

"Where did you get that idea?"

"When you see them on TV, they always look poor, and they talk poor. I was just wondering."

The long day of labor and now the heat of the shack combined with his full belly caused Bill to yawn with fatigue.

"Yeah, I've met a few," his father replied. He scratched the deepening stubble on his face and waited for the questions to come.

"What are they like?"

Not quite sure what his son was really trying to find out, he responded slowly, methodically, and deliberately. "Pretty much like anybody else, I guess. Trying to make a living, raise their kids," and after a short pause, "drink a little beer."

"A lot of people don't like black people."

"I know," his father slowly responded, pausing to look up at his son before extinguishing the lantern.

"There are a lot of good reasons to hate a man, but the color of his skin ain't one of them. Don't ever forget that son."

Seconds went by before he spoke again.

"Can you ever imagine how difficult it must be to get through a world where you're not liked, hell in some places not even tolerated. Not because you're a liar or a thief, or dangerous, but because of the color of your skin."

Bill had no idea that his father had given race any thought at all and was surprised by the passion that could be heard in his voice.

"Not being able to get a job or respect or send your kids to college just because of the color of your skin. What the hell is that?"

Ray slowly crawled from his bunk, opened the stove door, stirred the glowing ambers and added a few sticks of wood to the dying flames. After returning to the warmth of his sleeping bag, he resumed his recitation.

"I am so ashamed at what the white man has done to the black man in this country that I feel guilty every time I see a black man."

Minutes passed without a word being spoken. So quiet in his bunk for so long Ray suspected that his son had drifted off when he heard him roll to a more comfortable spot and clear his throat.

"How are you doing Bill?" fatherly concern showed in his voice, "You holding up alright?"

"I'm good Pop, I've got some sore muscles and I could use a bath but I'm doing okay. I'm learning a lot about beaver and deer." Bill paused for a moment before he continued, "I sure would like a bowl of ice cream though."

"I'll see to it that you get a whole box when we get out of here."

The stink from the kerosene lantern and the smoke tinged air from the stove when mixed with the unwashed smell of the two bodies in the close confines of the hut generated a smell that only a skunk could relate to.

Beyond the thin canvas walls the temperature of the black night continued to plummet.

Small talk between the two continued for a few minutes when Ray asked, "What have you been thinking about these last few days, hungry, cold and tired?"

"Dad…don't worry about me, I'm OK. This will be something I can tell my kids about, if I ever have kids." Stopping only a moment for reflection, "This is the most exciting thing that's ever happened to me. You know, the beaver, the cold, your cooking."

"Even more exciting than the night you spent in the woods?"

"That was another night I'll never forget."

"How you doing in school?"

"Do we have to talk about that?" Bill asked as he rolled up onto his side and pulled the sleeping bag up over his one cold exposed ear and nose.

"No, not if you don't want to."

"I'm not doing so good," Bill, replied, the sound of disgust in his voice. "I'm not very smart. Sometimes I think I am but when I get my tests back..." he let the rest of his thought die in the dark.

"Your smart enough," concern tinged his father's voice, "You just haven't figured it out yet. You will. You just keep plugging away; don't give up."

They were helpless remarks for a son he couldn't assist, and the advice seemed inadequate.

Ray had left school after the seventh grade and had never returned. He, too, had been a poor student and feared that his own inadequacies had shown up in his son. His only salvation had been his perseverance, his strong work ethic, and his willingness to take on any amount of hardship, like this one, to get ahead. His drive to "make a buck" had been his salvation.

That biting cold night and the nights that followed when there was little to do except talk, father and son explored values and beliefs.

At two in the morning Bill awoke with a start. His father roughly shook his shoulder. "Get up, there's something you should see." Pulling himself from his sleeping bag and sliding into his unlaced boots before draping his wool coat over his shoulders, Bill in perplexed silence followed his father out into the bitter still night.

"Take a look at that," he commanded, pointing into the northern sky. Nature was putting on a display of magnificence unlike anything he had ever seen.

Wafting curtains of yellow and green against a black star stippled sky, captivating in its beauty, mesmerized the two onlookers.

"Northern Lights," he whispered.

"Wow," was all that Bill could say in his quiet under breath. Undimmed by streetlights or headlights, the undulating fabric of space wafted and shimmered in the black night sky. They stood silently watching the celestial magnificence until driven back inside by the cold.

"What makes it, Pop?"

"What makes it?" he repeated." I'm not quite sure. It's all deep science to me, but I've read that stuff coming from the sun reacts with the magnetic poles of the earth. The south pole has the same thing apparently."

Once more curled into his warm nest Bill finally recognized the odd feelings that had nagged at his unconscious since his arrival. It was the aloneness, the desolation, so omnipresent as to be nearly palpable. Some men, he reasoned before he drifted off to sleep, feared aloneness, abhorred solitude, especially solitude of this magnitude. Others, like his father were attracted to it. His father was not like other men. He sought it out and embraced it. Bill realized that he was not like his father either. On the other hand, he had no fear of aloneness. He simply didn't mind it. What made the difference? He wondered. Was it his fathers' self-reliance or was it, perhaps, a deep distrust in other men? These were questions for another night.

He soon drifted into a dreamless sleep disturbed occasionally by the coldness of his nose, the only thing protruding from his heavily quilted sleeping bag.

The morning finally came numbing and penetrating in its ferocity. On the tree just beyond the door, red dyed mercury in the thermometer had pulled down into its bulbous base. At 22° below zero the air crackled with hardness and made it difficult to pull a breath. No beaver would be skinned without a fire. Today bare hands would go numb in minutes when handling a wet carcass. Before any beaver were pulled up through the ice, wood would have to be gathered and a fire built. The day would be gruelingly hard, movements would be slow and clumsy and the loads they carried would be more burdensome. Bill was certain that he had never experienced such bitterness.

"Put your sandwiches inside your long johns", his father instructed." Up close to your chest wall. That will keep them from freezing."

They struck out that morning moving along the shoreline of the Dead Cambridge, the outlet from "C" Pond, and worked their way up Lost Brook, building fires, and skinning beaver as they went. After they had exhausted the colonies that had been set the week before, they struck off west over a few low ridges and came upon another brook that the topography maps referred to as "Red Brook." They worked their way down to the set-up colonies and back to the Dead Cambridge. The beaver catch had far exceeded all expectations and the toboggan was becoming increasingly ponderous. As the muted sun began to edge its way toward the horizon, the two weary men headed for the camp across the open ice of "C" Pond. Constant movement was the only remedy against the temperature's onslaught.

They could hear the drone of the plane long before they saw it. Finally, skimming above the treetop, the single engine Cessna came into view. They squinted up through their own frosty breaths to recognize a game wardens air patrol. Ray waved and the plane tipped its wings in return recognition. It would be impossible for the plane to land with all the dead tree stumps protruding above the icy surface of the pond. Once more the plane circled low around the pond. One of the two occupants opened a side window, stuck a bullhorn out and in a booming electronically altered voice pronounced "thirty-eight below when we left Roxbury Pond this morning."

Ray waved his hand in appreciation that he understood the message. The plane tipped his wings once again before it banked and headed back toward Roxbury in the waning afternoon light.

"Who was that Pop?"

"The Game Wardens. John Swasey was one; I don't know who the other one was."

"How'd they know we were here?" The extra exertion of talking while walking showed in his labored breathing.

"I ran into John a couple of weeks ago and told him we were coming in here to trap."

"Why'd you tell him, Bill wanted to know?"

"Why not, just because he's in uniform doesn't make him the bad guy. You do know that, don't you?"

Bill studied his father's question for a few minutes. He had always considered a man in uniform as a policeman and stayed away from them. They were authority and all authority was to be avoided. But if his father confided personal things to an authority figure, then he supposed that all authority couldn't be bad.

"I wanted them to know we were in here just in case anything should happen."

"What can happen?"

"Oh, I don't know," his father conjectured, "your mother could shoot someone in the shop". The "shop" was Ray's euphemism for the bar.

Laboring their way back to the hut, Bill was forced to reconsider his thoughts of the night before. They weren't so all alone after all. His thoughts of complete isolation needed revision. Nobody was alone anymore, really alone at least not in the state of Maine.

"What's for supper," Bill wanted to know as they approached the camp, so cold and desolate appearing, enfolded as it was within the evergreens.

"Beans and hot dogs and I think some brown bread," said his father. Pausing long enough to remove his snowshoes, "Shouldn't take more than an hour or two to thaw."

The evening chores, besides the familiar ritual of building a fire and melting snow for water, included sharpening the skinning knives and making plans for the next day's activities.

"Pop, my butt itches something awful"

"After supper, we'll make a pot of hot water. We could both use a good quick scrub."

Bill found that anything he did with his pants off in zero-degree weather, he did in a hurry. It may have been one of the fastest scrub jobs in history, but the soapy hot water worked its magic and the rewards were remarkable. With clean shorts and a fresh tee shirt beneath the same smelly long johns, he felt better.

"Boy, will I sleep tonight," he remarked to his father as he settled into his sleeping bag.

"It's not as cold right now as it was this morning, do you think?" Bill inquired of his Dad as he traced his initials into the inch think frost that had accumulated on the canvas ceiling. Huge puffy formations of frost from his moist breath and hot bath water grew delicate tendrils of ice and needed to constantly be brushed from the walls and ceiling. But now the spindly needles were falling of their own accord as the warmth in the room began to build.

"OK lights out," spoke Ray as he reached out from the confines of his bunk to extinguish the lantern.

The two stirred around in the dark, looking for their comfort spot. Finding comfort Ray waited for some bombshell of a question that he was now certain would come. And then it came.

"Do you believe in God, Pop." Ray had always felt a bit uncomfortable talking about God. He had not grown up in a religious family and God was a taboo subject.

Nobody in his family had ever prayed or asked for heavenly help. If he wanted something done, he did it himself, and no prayer was going to help.

"Why do you ask?" Ray wanted to know.

In spite of Ray's lack of schooling or any formal education, he read extensively on his own, usually at night before he went to sleep. He read about the age of dinosaurs and rise of mankind, and logic convinced him that there was no God. There was no one to blame or credit for the way things were today.

"You and mom send me to Sunday School every Sunday, but you don't go yourself."

Ray felt the need to respond to his son's questions and knew that his answers must not hint of evasion. "You're going to make a lot of decisions in your life, about people, about politics, about religion, and a lot of other things. In order to make a sound decision on anything, you need to get as much information as you can. But, to answer your question, No, I don't believe in God and I believe even less in religion." Ray now found himself dangerously close to dictating how his son should think, and he didn't want to do that. "If you come to find, after you look at all the information, that you get comfort from God or religion, then I think you should embrace it." There was a short pause, as some pocket of pitch in the stove popped. "I just never did," he finally continued, "but I don't think you should make your decisions about what you believe or disbelieve based on what you hear from me."

"Religion is not a bad thing you understand. After all, the laws that we live by mostly come from the Bible and religion. But every once in a while, some nut comes along and tells people that he alone talks to God, and God talks back to him. Now I've got to tell you, that's a lot of horseshit. There are no ghosts in this world, holy or otherwise. And that guy Jesus, as far as I'm concerned, he was just a man, probably a good man who was totally fed up with a government that wouldn't do anything to help its people. I suspect he surrounded himself with some radicals who were trying to make a change just as he was. He was really good at it too, but that doesn't make him a god.

The camp went quiet for a while as Bill considered his father's logic. The only sounds came from within the stove where dry wood was giving up its energy.

"A kid at school asked me if I believed in God and I said yes. I think I felt guilty for not thinking like he did, so I lied."

"What do you mean you felt guilty", his father asked in an effort to keep his son talking.

"Well...like a sin or something, if I didn't believe."

"Son don't worry about it tonight. You've got lots of time."

"I figure," his father spoke in a resolute manner, that when I die, I'll go in the box and that's it. If I have any life after death, it's just the little bit of me that's in you. That's pretty much the end of things, if you ask me. Now roll over and get some sleep, we've got a big day tomorrow."

Tomorrow would be a slow, hardworking, return to camp number one day. In two days, Bill hoped they would be returning to civilization. Not that Bill was complaining about his life as a pioneer and trapper, he wasn't. But a hot soapy bath with water up to his neck was something he was looking forward to, that, and a home cooked meal. His mother was among the world's great cooks: and when he was away from home, he missed her and her cooking.

Sleep went pretty much undisturbed for Bill. Even the mouse was quiet. He heard his father get up once in the night. In the morning, they both realized that the vicious short-lived cold snap had abated. The monotonous gray somber skies however muted the usual splendor of the dawn and forebode an impending storm.

To Bill's surprise the evening conversations with his father had become the highlight of each exhausting day. He loved and idealized his father. He recognized in his father a source of endless information, and limitless stories filled with good humor and life's lessons. Knowing that his father had left school in the seventh grade only added to the admiration that he felt. He had entered the world without many of the tools needed to fight life's battles.

Some of the more philosophical ideas were lost on the thirteen-year-old, but those that sank in; he would carry for the rest of his life.

Largely self-taught Ray had taken a marginal business and turned it around. "Ray's Lunch" may not have turned into the restaurant that he had envisioned early on, but it had, after a few years of experimentation, become the nightspot to visit. With the vision to cater to soldiers returning from the war, he thrived where others survived. He found that with good help he could run the business and still satisfy his need to be in the woods. He couldn't let go of his roots.

He had been born the middle child of seven on a small farm in Back Kingdom, Maine. Game was plentiful in the forests surrounding the cleared pastures and hay fields of his fathers' farm. As soon as he was old enough to understand that a raccoon or fox fur could put a few dollars in his pockets, he made it his quest to become accomplished at catching them. He had learned to understand their habits and trick them into getting caught. He was so good at trapping, that within a few years he was considered to be among the best.

When he had completed the seventh grade, his father ordered him to quit school. "I need more help on the farm." From that time on Ray worked on the farm for his board and room and schemed how he would get out from under his father's thumb. At seventeen, he left home, determined to make his own way. For a few years, he beat around on construction, until he landed a job in the local paper mill. His job in the mill was steady, secure and decent paying, but his passion was always the woods. It took some years but seeing the closing days of the war in sight, he knew it could be his great opportunity to get ahead. Bill had heard the stories and had witnessed his father's driving ambition.

Ray's nest egg of savings grew along with his maturity, and when he made the decision to get into a business of his own, he went on the hunt. After several months of fruitless searching, he found, through a rumor, what he was looking for. Appraising real estate, borrowing money and dealing with a lawyer was a whole new world, but he quickly adapted.

Jimmy Caliendo had come over from the old country and had made his living as a barber. From all accounts, it had been a decent living, but it hadn't been easy. When the depression struck in '29 his business, like all businesses, suffered. In 1933 when prohibition was lifted, he added a bar to his barbershop and began selling beer along with his haircuts. It seemed logical. A beer and a haircut, two bits. They went together like beans and hot dogs. It worked well; Jimmy had a good steady business and an ideal location. In the closing days of the war Jimmy was getting older and tired. Rumor had it that Jim was in a mood to sell his business, building and all. Ray finally struck a deal after several bouts of Yankee haggling. All that he needed now was to come up with the money.

Old man Ferguson, the president of the local bank told him, "don't even bother to fill out the paperwork. You have no collateral, your home is mortgaged, and you have no business experience. We won't be lending you any money."

In desperation, he went to his father who agreed to a loan at six percent, and a second note on the house he and Helen had bought a few years earlier. Making a deal with the devil seemed his only option, so he took it. The paperwork was all nice and legal, signed by a lawyer, and on the day of the sale, Ray went to his father for the money. "I don't trust no banks" he said as he led his son to the cellar. Ray watched his old man dig a hole in the ground and retrieved a rusty coffee can choked with cash. Back upstairs at the kitchen table, five thousand dollars exchanged hands.

Later that day in his lawyer's office as Ray counted the money onto the desk, his barrister, curled his nose in repugnant disgust, cried, "Where in the hell did you dig this up, it stinks!" The musty disagreeable smell of the damp cellar earth clung desperately to the bills. That's how Ray got his beer joint.

. The last day's work began as they all had, laboriously. Trudging ahead of the toboggan they made their way along the shore of the pond before striking off to the east. Pulling the last remaining traps, spread out as they were, would take all the daylight hours. The skins that had been harvested so far were stacked like frozen cordwood beside camp number one. Today's catch would be the last. It's a good thing, Bill thought. Any more skins and the load would become too heavy to haul. The day's work went well. The harvest of skins was added to the accumulating burden on the toboggan.

The sky's thickening turgidity enveloped and nearly obliterated the noon light, casting a twilight pall on a colorless world. The drabness of the day, however foreboding, couldn't suppress the building excitement in Bill's brain for the planned early morning departure. Throughout the day his ordinarily high spirits were a bit extraordinary. He had had enough of the trapper's world. The enthusiasm of a week ago, had dampened. The early American trappers that he loved to read about must have lived a hard, even a bleak existence. A fact in conspicuous omission in the stories he enjoyed. His scalp itched, as did his privates. The experience and the comradery with his father had been wonderful and enlightening, but he was tired. He craved uninterrupted sleep in a warm bed without the company of a mouse.

How Lewis and Clark had withstood the hardships of crossing a continent; how Sacagawea a nineteen-year-old girl, carrying an infant had endured the three-year trek defied his imagination.

One o'clock witnessed the fluttering first flakes of what would become the worst winter storm in ten years. Haste became the hallmark of the day's labor.

"Looks like we're in for a good one Pop," Bill said, casting his glance skyward, referring to the gathering storm.

"Good one hell, we just might have trouble getting out of here."

"How much trouble?" asked Bill, his father's ominous words raising concern in his mind. He had gone ahead of his father and pulled several carcasses onto the ice and laid them in a row. He had cut the tails off and made circular incisions about the paws in an effort to help speed the skinning process.

"Oh well, we can get out, if that's what you're asking, but it could become an all-day job, and maybe half the night as well." The snow was coming fierce now in a hard slant pattern that obscured visibility to within a few yards. His eye lashes and brows would catch and hold the delicate driving flakes, obscuring his vision and turning his view of the landscape into some ghostly aberration.

They were winding down now—thank god—and tomorrow morning they would be leaving. Prudence told Ray that they should pack and leave right now. Snow had been falling since early afternoon and now at dark, there was six inches of snow on the ground with no sign of letting up. Working all day, they had pulled twenty–two beaver from the ice, most of them big. They all were heavy and now both the Ray and his son were exhausted from the day's labors. They had cut more than thirty holes through the ice; ice that had grown in thickness each day and was now up to fifteen inches. Pelts had been removed from carcasses, rolled, tied and made ready for transport. A hundred and ten hides in all, more than they could have hoped for and not, he hoped, more than they could haul. After this exhausting day, there was no chance of attempting the walk tonight. Ray was stronger than his son and knew he would struggle to make the trip. It would be a bad trade off all around. In the morning, they would be rested, but the new snow would be a foot or more and harder going. The unthinkable, leave the pelts behind, not one chance in hell. So, in the morning, they would go, in spite of the snowfall.

"Pop, I've never seen anything like it. Man, it's coming down." In no mood for idle chatter at this moment, he instructed his son on loading and balancing the toboggan, and the packsacks. Tomorrow would be a long hard day.

His son had done everything and more that had been asked of him. He had more than held up his end. Without complaints, Bill had reached the end of each day at the frazzled end of his endurance. As a father, he'd felt remorse for bringing him, subjecting him to this strength-sapping ordeal, but he was grateful to see the qualities that his son possessed. Bill had endured the hardships, the cold and the labors without a serious complaint and at the end of each exhausting day had found the energy and the inquisitiveness to ask an endless stream of questions.

"Don't set anything down" Ray instructed Bill. "At this rate, anything you set down will be covered in minutes. Lost forever."

Kicking their feet clear and brushing snow from their pants, the two trappers entered the shack.

"God it's black in here."

"Cold too," Bill said. The kerosene lantern cast an eerie subdued smoky gloom about the room; the ceiling and floors were wet; Congealed but not fully frozen. The moisture and the mixture of pine straw and ash from the stove gave off a rancid odor that assaulted the senses. During the days' absence droplets from the ceiling had frozen producing pencil like icicles with tiny droplets falling from their tips. Wetness had run down the inside walls froze into lacy mirror like sheets. Every movement of the two men caused the walls to waft. The shattered glaze rained down onto everything.

"Hey, Pop," Bill suggested, crinkling his nose in disgust, "why don't we just burn it when we leave."

"What are you, nuts," his father said with a grin as he kindled the tiny flame in the tin stove. "I'll come back in the spring when the roads dry out and get all this stuff."

Within minutes heat from the stove could be felt up around the ceiling and both men began to remove their outer garments.

"What's for supper?" Bill asked.

"Steak and beans."

"Steak?"

"Yah, I've been saving them, and hiding them for tonight. It's our last night in this little corner of paradise. Next week we'll sell tickets. First prize gets a week in here. Second prize gets two weeks."

They sat and talked about the upcoming trip back to civilization. They savored the steaks that had been Pan-fried in the confines of the camp. The air had become smoky and aroma filled. The cramped quarters were further compromised by the raging storm outside. Packsacks normally left outside were brought in to keep them from being buried and to facilitate a quick start in the morning. The hardships of the chores were more so with the added burden of the ever-deepening snows, by days' end fatigue had burrowed deep into joints and muscles. Bill had a spot on the front of each shoulder that he would press into and kneed with the tip of one index finger. The stabbing pain was made worse by the pressure, oddly it felt deliciously awful to make it hurt. Repeatedly he would torture the spot, failing to understand his need to illicit the pain.

Dishes were cleaned, the camp's interior was put to rights and the two made ready to climb into their bunks. "Did I ever tell you about the time I caught another trapper stealing a beaver out of my trap?"

"No," Bill perked up, "what happened?"

"Well," Ray began as he extinguished his pipe, tapping the bowl of ash onto the floor, "I had set up a colony on Saunders Pond; I was the only one in there." I had found that bunch of beaver the summer before. Anyway, there was this other trapper, his name was Ray also. He followed my tracks in and set it up too. He came into the shop one night early and gets a beer. He says he was up in Saunders Pond that day to check his traps and thought he'd check mine, "you know, as a favor."

That got my attention, because if there is one rule, you never touch another man's traps.

"So, what happened," inquired Bill, as he climbed into his bunk.

"I questioned him a little. 'Raymond, I said, did you get anything?' He said that he hadn't but that I had a kitten in one of mine, you know Bill's father explained, a young beaver. I didn't think too much more about it at the time. He drank his beer and left. But about two hours later his brother-in-law comes through the door looking for a beer. This guy knows I trap and says to me, I was up to Ray's earlier and he had just caught one of the biggest blanket beaver that I had ever seen. You can imagine how that really caught my attention." Ray grimaced, I remember the moment like it was yesterday. "The next morning, I was on the road before daylight. I was determined to find out just exactly what took place." Ray was a great storyteller and knew how to keep his listener's rapt attention.

"As soon as I got onto the trail, I knew something was screwy. I could see his snowshoe trail where he had gone in the morning before, but there was no sign of his coming back out.

When I got to the pond, I cut my trap out of the ice, and sure enough I had this little kitten of a beaver. I noticed two things right off. One, he had pulled all his traps out; he was gone. And two, the kitten in my trap had a deep trap mark on its other front paw, the one that wasn't in my trap. What he had done, the dumb son-of-a-bitch, he caught the kitten and when he cut my trap out, I had the blanket. So, he swaps. The only problem, he's so stupid, he put the wrong paw in my trap."

Bill, by this time is antsy with anticipation visualizing the story as it unfolds.

"I did a little more snooping around and found where he had disposed of some chunks of ice embedded with hair. There was some more ice with hair around my trap. There's no question he pulled a big beaver out of my trap."

"So, Pop, how come there wasn't any trail of him coming out?"

"There was a trail alright, but it went down the backside of the mountain, through the woods, two miles longer, but it eventually came out in the same place, where his car was parked."

"Why do you suppose he did that?"

"Simple," Ray said, "he was scared that he might meet me on the trail coming in to check my traps, while he was on the way out. He knew he'd have trouble explaining what went on up there, so he tried to sneak out the back way. Dumb bastard!"

"Did you ever confront him?"

"I called him up. Told him that I knew what he did, but he just lied about it. I told the game wardens what he'd done, but there was nothing they could do." Ray paused for a few minutes to collect his thoughts. The hot stove would occasionally snap and then he continued. "They said he'd pulled crap like that before. A couple years later he shot a man in the woods, mistook the guy for a deer. He left the guy in the woods to die but they caught him through ballistics, and a witness who saw him in the area. They couldn't prove that he knew that he had shot someone, but he was never allowed a license to hunt or trap again."

Not yet ready to let the story end, Bill had to ask, "Did you ever see him again?"

"I saw him walking down Congress Street six months later. When he spotted me, he turned and ran like a rabbit. One thing for sure," he grinned with his understated laugh, "he never came into the shop for another beer. I lost a customer and a blanket beaver on that deal."

Chapter 6

THE LONG WALK

Nearly a foot and a half of snow had fallen in the night and it had been a chore to force the door open. Since the storm began nearly two feet of snow had fallen. The accumulation against the out-swinging door, like a buttress, was formidable. Kicking and nudging and warming the air with invectives, Ray finally forced a gap wide enough for the slimmer Bill to squeeze through.

Bill stood in the dark, his eyes closed. Silhouettes of the trees and giant boulders were nearly indefinable. The silence of the woods was hardly intruded upon by the quiet whisper of falling snow. Individually uncountable and nearly weightless as the fine geometric crystals fell in silence. Collectively they generated a nearly indiscernible hiss. His father's expletive broke the spell along with his last-minute rummaging inside the shack.

"I told you that I'd save your life on this trip," too gleeful he expounded, "Without me you probably would have starved to death. They would have found your poor starved body in the spring, locked in your tomb of death. Thank me, Pop."

"Thank you, now shut up and eat," jokingly responded the older man. "You had better get that foolishness out of your system right now. I don't think you'll feel so cute in about four hours."

"It's going to be tough, isn't it?"

"I'm afraid so. To lighten the mood somewhat, Ray changed the subject. "But I'll be glad to get you home for a bath. You stink."

With both their clothing and skin wreaking of kerosene, the rancid fetid stench of beaver fat, the musty tang of wood smoke, and the accumulated six-day essence of body odor, neither the man nor his son was a bed of roses.

Snow had fallen unabated through the night. It had become a looming difficulty to the trip home. "It looks to be falling at about two inches an hour," Ray surmised. With no end in sight, each succeeding minute only made things worse. Getting onto the trail soon was requisite. Breaking trail through two feet of fresh snow on snowshoes would be formidable. The toboggan loaded with over a hundred and fifty pounds of frozen hides only made the job that much harder. Ray carried another fifty pounds in the pack basket strapped to his back, and Bill was carrying an additional forty or fifty pounds as well. Ray attached two ropes to the front of the toboggan and one at the rear. Pulling together they eased the strain on each, but it proved to be tricky largely a matter of timing. As they struck out, Bill cast a backward glance to the forlorn shack. Nearly invisible in the predawn murk.

He had learned so much here. He had learned the hard rules of men in a hard world. He had been given a glimpse into a world he was just coming into. A hardness of the mind, the will, and their necessity for survival. These lessons for living had been taught to him by his father in an unforgetting classroom. Bill also had gleaned an insight into the fairness of his father who possessed a hard, fair generosity, but one not to be taken for granted. His father had labored far harder than he had. He had carried more than his share of the load, and yet had never spoken a cross word to him. hand, Bill had been made to understand that he was expected to contribute to his utmost, and he hoped that he had measured up.

"Today, won't be easy," his father said.

The obviousness of his prediction, based on the weight they would be pulling, the depth of the snow plus the loads on their backs required no response, but Bill had to ask:

"You mean some parts of this trip have been easy?'

"That's right," replied his father.

"I'd like to know what part?"

"All of it, son. Compared to what lays ahead today. All of it."

Within a mile father and son had gotten the timing down pat, and the heavy muscle-straining load lumbered slowly along. On steep descents and long downgrades Bill would remove his harness, move to the rear of the sled, hook back up and provide the breaking necessary to keep his father from being run over. The morning went slow but trouble free. The loads were barely manageable. More beaver had been caught then Ray could have hoped for. He and Bill knew they were in for a hard day. The twenty-four inches of snow on the ground at six a.m., became deeper by noon.

The perversity of the pull gently eased with the downward direction of the trail into a long valley. By the time the trail's length had been halved, shoulder sockets felt as though they had separated, and their haunches pained to touch. With each quarter hour of unrelenting labor came a well-earned respite. As the day moved forward even the fifteen-minute periods began to diminish.

The canvas knapsack that Bill carried on his back lacked the structural rigidity of a pack basket and the frozen hides within protruded in knobby clots. Clothing offered little protection. Bill's skin was chafed and the underlying bone, where muscle attached was tortured. The lesser weight of the fabric bag was more than compensated for by the terrible discomfort that it generated. Both Ray and his son had their burdens to bear.

The gray sky, low, overcast and thick with falling flakes barely became lighter from dawn through noon and just as unnoticeably darkened as the day began to wane. Their strength ebbed with the day. Exertion narrowed their fields of vision to the immediate. The next step of the next yard was all they recognized of the next mile. The drudge, the fatigue, and the relentless repetition erased memory. A day later Bill could not recall a conversation or an incident that would hallmark any hour of that day. Slowly one foot dogged another making "vanishing tracks" in the uncompromising topography. Their tracks were quickly lost beneath billowing drifting snow.

"How much longer?" gasped Bill as they sat side by side on an old blow down that bordered the trail?

Ray paused to light his beat-up briar and allow his back and legs a bit of respite before he answered. Finally, he expelled a lung full of the aromatic smoke, "Not much further now."

"God, I hope not," came his son's agonized breathless reply. "Cause I ain't got much left" He gasped at the air, trying to reduce the oxygen debt he had been building all day.

"It's dark Pop," he spoke with sudden realization, "I can hardly see the trail."

"I know," reassured his father, "but it won't be long. Less than a mile, I think. But," he added, "from here to the top of East B Hill it's all up hill.

By this time the sandwiches and the candy bars were long gone. They were eating snow by the handful and sucking on icicles when they could be found to replace fluids lost through perspiration and labored breathing. And still it snowed.

Like a mirage in a dark mist, the outline of the jeep slowly came into view. The pair labored the heavy sleigh up and over the final ascent into the middle of the clearing that once was the road. It would once again be a county road, come the spring, when the snows melted away. Now, however, at seven in the evening the fall of new snow was above thirty inches. The jeep had set for a week in its icy cache and appeared more like a giant wedding cake under a two-foot blanket of frosty icing.

In the rear confines of the vehicle were stored or thrown a miscellaneous of tools, chains, a shovel, and junk. "I never throw anything out. You never know when you're going to need something."

Loading the rolled frozen skins into the back of the jeep would be priority "one" after the jeep was started and the tiny heater put to the test.

With a broom and the shovel Ray pushed and swept the snow from around, and off the roof of the jeep. The stout little workhorse of a jeep was completely immersed in a cocoon of snow. The accumulation was now so high it had coalesced with that which had fallen onto the hood and roof. In the front, ground snow had aggregated above the headlights and met the overhanging snow from the hood which itself extended back and up the windshield joining that from the roof. Nature's camouflage was complete. Bill knew the jeep to be hidden there but until his father swept away the obfuscating over cover, he could only accept that fact on faith.

The frozen shackles and springs snapped and groaned as Ray settled into the hard, cold shiny seat. The well-worn key retrieved from the ashtray, just where he had left it, slid loosely into its sheath.

Pulling the hand activated choke and beating a tattoo on the gas pedal he turned the key expecting that the little four-cylinder engine would cough to life.

For nearly a week the jeep had stood alone sentinel to the trappers' departure. Through a cold snap that reduced steel to the brittleness of glass, and oil to the viscosity of black strap, the battery simply lacked the power to turn the engine. Even the explosiveness of gasoline in the intense chill had lost some of its combustibility. The only response he got from the starter was a low guttural growl, a snarl that had no teeth.

Bill sat helplessly atop the mountain of frozen hides nearly catatonic with fatigue, occasionally wiping his red rheumy nose along his sleeve leaving a shiny frozen ribbon between his elbow and wrist.

As Ray exited the vehicle Bill asked without the strength to care. "What are we going to do now?"

Warm and exhausted from his recent exertions Bill fought the overpowering urge to sleep where he sat. It was coming on to the dead of night and they had been on the move since before daylight. He had nothing left to give. His head lolled; his eyes refused his commands to stay open. He heard nothing of his father's mutterings or exertions. Time ceased to be a factor in Bills brain as one system after another began to shut down. Sometime later, he had no idea how much later, he was rudely, roughly shaken back to consciousness.

"Come on, get up, time to load these skins." Above the volume of his father's voice he could hear the steady, high-pitched throb of the jeep's engine.

"You got it going!"

"It wasn't easy"

"How?"

"You do know what I use for antifreeze in this old jeep, don't you?"

"Is this a trick question?".

"Antifreeze, I guess."

"I use kerosene." Ray said.

Incredulously the son looked to the father, "Nah. You're joking."

"I'm telling you."

"Can you do that, without it blowing up or something?" Bill was suspicious and uncertain of his father's forth coming explanation.

"Unlike gasoline," he informed his son; it doesn't explode, it burns and because it doesn't freeze it makes good anti-freeze. I took a piece of tin from the back and shaped it into a pan. I then drained off some kerosene from the radiator, put my handkerchief in the pan for a wick and built a fire under the block. In ten minutes, the engine was warm, and it started right up."

"Come on," Ray commanded. "We've still got some work to do. We've got to clear snow out from the front of the tires."

"Christ, there's two feet of snow on the ground, if the jeep can't get through it, then we're going to have to walk"

"How far?"

"It's about five miles to the plowed road."

"Oh Pop" wailed Bill, pleading; "I don't think I can do it."

"You can do what you have to do. You wanted to take this trip, remember? So quit your bitching and help. What in the hell do you think…that you're going to stay?"

Pulling himself out of his own pool of pity, Bill finally answered "No, I'm sorry Pop."

Once the frozen hides had been loaded it was plain to see that the springs had bottomed out and the jeep's body was resting firmly on its axles. Both temper and lethargy had dissipated under the labor of moving the cargo of frozen hides.

"If weight will give us traction then we should be all set," Ray said, again showing a bit of humor in his voice.

The new snow, light and fluffy, was beat and shoveled from in front of the wheels and far enough down the road to give the vehicle a running start.

The defroster and heater pumped out tiny ribbons of heat that coated the interior of the windshield with a translucent patina of condensation. Half blind by the clouded glass and the still falling flakes, Ray forced the tiny workhorse forward.

For several hundred yards the gutsy little machine muscled its way along the buried roadway until its tires finally lost their traction. Repeatedly Ray would grab the shovel, dig snow from under the frame and clear a path ahead. By the time that they made it down the mountain to the plowed roads, the storm had abated completely. Bill had grabbed the shovel to help a few times but weakened and nearly prostate he was no longer much help. Two days later, Bill was back at school, following an unstoppable eating-sleeping binge.

Over the course of the next few weeks the skins were stretched, debrided of all the fatty tissue and after a period of drying, were ready for market. Local fur buyers knew of the large catch and came around to make their offers. Unfortunately, the fluctuating price of fur was in a downtrend and profits from the expedition were less than expected. Never again did Ray and the now recovered Henry embark on such an onerous undertaking.

The following year the partnership between Ray and Henry fell by the wayside. Ray still trapped beaver but not with the same zest. The price for good beaver pelts had dropped away and he began to take aim at a new adversary, the Eastern Coyote, whose migratory patterns were making inroads into the Maine backcountry. The demand for their beautiful, silky, gray and black fur was on the rise. His friendship with Henry remained strong, however, and from time to time they found themselves competing for beaver in the same colonies.

Bill never trapped that way again, but that week in the woods with his father gave him memories that lasted a lifetime. He had stories to tell his grandchildren and on cold blustery winter nights sixty years later, he would sit before the fire, nurse his glass of bourbon, and remember one of the times of his life.

Chapter 7

FARM LIFE

Five miles north of town on the west bank of the Swift River in the tiny settlement of Hale the Edmond's farm was slowly being reclaimed by nature. The once white paint, peeled, blistered, and chipped away through years of neglect, and now lay along the granite slab foundation in speckled, eroded flakes. The empty buildings were clustered together along the western edge of the long narrow valley. Worked by the Edmond's family for more than one hundred and fifty years the farm was well known in the area for its intriguing history.

Prior to the Civil War the once prosperous farm had been a stop along the Underground Railroad. Southern blacks on their escape route to Canada and freedom would stop at the farm for rest and resupply. The Edmond's family lost ownership of the property in the nineteen thirties but the family name stuck. Several owners since then had exploited its dwindling assets and moved on. The wood had been cut, the stone and gravel had been quarried and finally some of the hand-hewn beams of the antiquated barns had been removed and sold for their aesthetic value.

Bill's mother had described the place as "going to rack and ruin."

A year and a half after their memorable C-Pond trapping expedition, Bill turned sixteen and his father bought the farm that Benjamin Edward's had carved from the wilderness. The bar that Ray had owned since the closing days of W.W.II no longer suited him. He had bought the bar as thousands of young men were returning from Europe and the South Pacific. They had all been thirsty and in search of getting on with their lives. Business had been good, and he had made good money, but now he wanted to get out. The hectic nightlife no longer suited him. Ray and Helen needed a quieter more peaceful way to make a living; a place in the country seemed to be a perfect choice.

Bill didn't care a great deal about where he lived, but the strange stone carvings about the place about the home and barns intrigued him. Within weeks of moving to the old farmhouse, he made an inquiry at the town library. Miss Berdeen, a fixture as permanent as the library building itself, took an instant liking to the boy and his inquisitiveness. She graciously helped him in his search.

Apparently one black family on their flee northward stopped at the farm and stayed. Evidence of their existence remained in one ancient photograph; African suns and other tribal symbols could be found about the place where they had been chiseled into the stone of chimneys and rock walls. Over a stone archway leading up to the front door of the main house rested a great carved stone head, whose Negroid features could not be denied. While the black man was doing his carving the owner, Edmonds, was doing a little carving of his own. Giant granite boulders set upright in the ground were polished smooth and chiseled with the complete text of the Ten Commandments and the Lord's Prayer. Other stones with biblical quotes, partially erased by years of erosion, were scattered about the farm. Benjamin Edmonds even had the foresight to carve his own gravestone that still stood in a small cemetery on the property.

With the profits from the sale of the bar Ray had renovated the one hundred and fifty-year-old structures into state-of-the-art poultry barns. Once a haven for field mice the dilapidated barns were rejuvenated, modernized and mechanized. When finished they contained more than eighty–five thousand chickens and one Jersey cow. The cow was Bill's, to feed, to care for and to milk.

Working alongside his father and a couple of "beer joint" carpenters, Bill had become a part of the barn's transformation.

Under his father's watchful eye and guiding hand, he had helped in the replacement of the busted foundations, and twisted walls. Roofs too were brought back into alignment, and the work helped Bill to erase his fear of heights.

The labor-intensive work went on for months and like most projects in this part of the country a close watch was kept on the expenses. Ray, with an astute eye for savings, scouted the country for a bargain. The sheet metal roof came from an old barn being razed in Dixfield; the roof was gotten for the price of removing it. The massive boiler, to heat his barns, came from Livermore Falls, fifty miles away. The great cast iron hulk with its many sections had gone through a conflagration and now stood, a rusting heap surrounded by ash, charred timber, and under three feet of snow just waiting to be dismantled and hauled away. He bought it all for the bargain price of two hundred and fifty dollars.

Ray had a way of coaxing the best from the men who worked for him. Among the "bar room" laborers there was great talent. Carpenters, an electrician, even a mechanical engineer, all of whom had lost their way at the bottom of a bottle. As a work force these men were not always dependable. Payday on Saturday was often followed by a no show on Monday with a lost long weekend in between.

Slowly the electrical wires were run, the plumbing installed, the furnace reassembled, and the structures rebuilt. All was accomplished for the price of a dollar an hour. Bill's labor was free. "Shove those damn planks up here, "became the battle cry around which Bill's summer seemed to revolve. Each epithet was accompanied with a grin from his father that in no way lessoned the urgency of the command. There was a lot of grinning that long intense summer. By fall the work was nearing completion.

Bill's education during this whole complicated convoluted process, soared. Working with talented, knowledgeable, likable guys; guys who could do anything except stay sober, guys who had sacrificed everything for a drink; guys who used the Kings English in ways he never thought possible, opened up his consciousness to a world he never knew existed. These men who, ate when they could, slept where they fell, and drank when they had a dollar to spend, talked to Bill about the evils of drink, even while planning to get drunk that night.

Spending time and working with these hard luck acquaintances of his father, turned out to be one long course in practical applied learning. Bill paid close attention, and exhibited no shyness around Elwee, Pee Wee and Sye. Running wire, connecting it to the proper wire, and threading pipe and all the other mysteries of construction were gladly passed along to Bill. He was a boy in the company of men, and they treated him accordingly. He was always the butt of any ribald bit of humor. But it wasn't all work. The man playfully tormented him with questions that made him blush.

"Hey Bill, you get a little poon last night?"

"What does that mean?"

"Poon Tang, boy. You've got to catch up" or maybe," Hey Bill, did you get your wick wet?"

"Will you guys shut up. I'm trying to get some work done." He didn't let the chatter bother him beyond the embarrassment. It was all in fun. He knew he was a target because of his youth.

Pee Wee Brown, Elwee Gallant, and Sye McCormick, were but a few of the abject lessons. They were the end result of a lifetime of drink, a road that Bill did not want to travel. Pee Wee, by his own admission began drinking at fourteen or fifteen and never stopped. At twenty-eight he looked to be fifty and was all used up. Ray Faulkner came home from the war with an English bride and never took a sober breath thereafter. Not even when the bride left, the house was taken, and the good mill job was gone.

McCormick, an engineer who had picked up the nickname Sye, had once worked on great projects in Washington, D.C., and New York City, and was now reduced to wiring a used furnace in a bargain basement chicken barn on a country road in Mexico, Maine. A fall from grace.

Learning, Bill realized was not always accomplished from the positive side of the equation. It was easier to see where the road was headed when seen from the finish line. His father's guidance and teaching by example wasn't always easy. It was always fair. He saw himself slowly becoming a man with the tools of self-reliance that came with the privilege.

That winter he worked caring for the chickens in the barns, hunted rabbit with his dog Susie, and becoming more attentive at school. In the late winter his father offered up a suggestion that wasn't a suggestion at all.

"If we get a cow will you take care of her?" asked his father one day.

"What do you mean take care of her," asked Bill with a wary eye, knowing for sure he wouldn't like the answer, and knowing for sure he couldn't say no to his father?

"You know what I'm talking about," the grin of his mouth, and the twinkle of his hazel eyes, used as weapons to assert his way "milk her morning and night; feed her." To sweeten the deal he added, almost as an afterthought. "I'll make the cottage cheese and the butter, and we'll split any profit."

The thought of a way to put a little money in his pocket did the trick and as the weather warmed they went shopping for a cow.

That's how Bill came to own a Jersey cow he affectionately named Molly. He came to love that cow the way his few friends might love their dog.

Morning and night without fail he punctually tended to her needs. He made butter and cottage cheese, which he sold when he put the sign along the road. The only respite he got from his self-imposed schedule occurred during the three months leading up to Molly's, dropping her calf, and the evening milking during football season.

In a compromised agreement with his father, Bill was allowed to play a sport, "Any one sport". Sports were not Bill's forte. He recognized his shortcomings. He lacked that innate ability to coordinate unrelated movements; field events were out of the question. He lacked the speed for track or the endurance for cross-country. Basketball with its endless repetition up and down the court did not appeal to him. His size and strength lent itself to football, but his lack of agility relegated him to the interior line. A position that was okay by him. He enjoyed the competition of play and enjoyed the comradery with his teammates even more.

Farm life was enjoyable to Bill. The work fit well into the cadence of his life and Sundays were all his own. He found sanctuary among the hay bales high up in the barn, where early afternoon sun streamed through a dusty gabled window. Steeped in the aroma of dried hay he delved into the unseen world of books. As a non-discretionary reader, he devoured anything in print. Dostoyevsky introduced him to Russia just as Dumas and Hugo allowed him to peak into early French history and its society. Churchill's volumes on the war captivated his attention and imagination for months. He found Mark Twain delightful. Hitler's lunatic ravings and Marx's treatise on capitalism opened up new avenues of thought. He read, enjoyed and marveled at the brilliance of some men's minds and the depravity of others.

In spite of his vast and varied readings his grades showed only modest improvement. He struggled to just maintain a passing grade.

"Bill, have you read An American Tragedy"? His friend Gene asked, rushing up to him in study hall.

"By Dreiser"?

"I don't know; I guess so".

"Yah, I read it, why"?

"I've got to turn in a book report this afternoon. Tell me what's it about?"

"You might not want me telling you. I gave a report on it last fall. I got a D"

"I don't care" scoffed Gene, "I need something on paper, and I need it in about two hours," he said checking his watch.

"OK, but don't blame me if you get a lousy grade," Bill said as he launched into an abbreviated narrative of a long psychologically motivated thriller.

About a week following that conversation, Gene rushed up to Bill in the hall and shook his hand, "Thanks man."

"For what?" asked Bill?

"That book report, man, I got an A."

"So, what's new," Bill admonished himself. "I read it and I got a D. I tell the story to a guy that hasn't read it, and he gets an A."

"Go figure."

In spite of the responsibilities of his cow, the chickens, the sale of butter and cheese, and the secreted time to read, he found more time than ever to spend in the woods. Mother Nature was right out his back door. Oh, the joy!

Rabbit hunting was now that close and Mitchell's sawdust pile was almost within walking distance, Ponds, lakes, rivers and brooks still had their allure, trout, bass, and wintertime pickerel were there for the taking, and by now Bill had his driver's license.

Early in the spring, within days of the ice "going out," a unique fishing trip would get underway.

"What do you say we go smelting tonight," Ray suggested to his still half-asleep son as they drank their morning coffee.

"You bet!" Bill nearly shouted in gleeful response." No school tomorrow and I sure don't have anything better to do."

"Alright then, get your work done and we'll go."

"Where are we going to go, Pop?"

"Indian Rock, I think, you know where, up in Oquossoc."

Indian Rock is an immense slab of granite deposited where it lay as the last ice-age glacier receded twenty thousand years ago. With one edge resting along the shore of a narrow channel where the Rangeley and the Mooselookmeguntic Lakes come together, the rock gently sloped down into the water. Running out of the Rangeley to their spawning grounds the smelts must slip past Indian Rock. It was here on this rock, the narrowest point of the channel that the men and women line up to take their turn and try their luck.

Smelts are a small feed fish that lives in the lakes and ponds, and in early spring they migrated up brooks and streams to spawn. Not more than four to five inches long, they are a good feed fish for the land-locked salmon and lake trout. They were also a great feed fish for a teen-age fisherman and his parents.

At four in the afternoon and only a week since the ice had "gone out" of the Lakes, the two struck out for Rangeley and the Rock. Along the way, the jeep approached a turn off toward Garland Pond, Ray slowed and took the turn. This beat-up gravel road would not take them to Rangeley, but Bill's father suddenly had something else on his mind.

"Where we going?" Bill asked, righting himself after the unprepared for detour.

"I thought we might take a look in around Philips brook, you know, where it empties into Garland Pond."

"That brooks only two feet wide, there's no smelts in there."

"Well, you never know."

When the migration was on, their paths up stream could become chocked dark with the darting tiny fish. A fine meshed net was used to "dip" them from the water. Like teenagers they seldom mated before midnight, but the capriciousness of nature being what it is, they had been known to make their run during the day.

The season lasted for only a few short weeks; some nights they "ran"; some nights, not. When the dipping was good, and the dipper was in the right place he might bring up a pint or more of the small succulent fish in a single pass of the net.

On a poor night he may bring up only a few at a time, often working until dawn in the early spring chill to fill a gallon jug.

Bill was never allowed to go smelting on a school night. Things were just too unpredictable.

Favorite spots like Indian Rock in Oquossoc, known for its great runs were often scattered with empty whiskey bottles; remnants of medicine to ward off the night chill. Occasionally, a carnival like atmosphere would materialize with a line of men waiting their turn to dip their net. Often more colds than fish were caught.

Garland Pond was different. The small body of water covering not more than five or six acres and was off the beaten path.

Bill considered the detour a waste of time; Philips Brook was narrow enough for a man to step across and in places nearly choked with high grass and alders. Aptly described as a drizzle of water it was thought by Bill to be a good place to catch a cold, and not much else.

By the time Ray and Bill, with the long-handled net slung over a shoulder, pushed through these obstacles to the brooks edge, the sun had set behind the mountainous ridges that surrounded the small pond. Casting a beam of light from his five-cell flashlight, the same one he used to jack deer, he found to his astonishment a black and silver iridescent shimmer reflecting from the bottom. Ray immediately doused the light, and, in a whisper, that could be heard for a hundred feet, "Get the buckets, they're running hot."

Knowing his father for the jester he could be "You're full of crap."

"No, I'm not, now get ready, I'm going to make a dip."

The flashlight was off, but some visibility remained from the waning day.

Finding a spot to dip the net and at the same time keep his knees dry, he knelt, choked up on the handle and gently swept the submerged net along the bottom hoping the smelts would run straight in. The maneuver could not have worked better. He lifted the net nearly brimming with hundreds of the gyrating, flaying fish; many cascading over the hoop topped net, falling back into the stream. They were the lucky ones who would continue up the brook, spawn and sow the seeds for next year's harvest. Lifting two to three quarts with every dip it took practically no time at all to fill the pair of ten-quart pails they had brought.

"God, Pop it's not even dark yet and we've got more than our limit. What are we going to do?"

"We're going to beat our ass for home. The game wardens won't be checking cars yet, and if we get onto the main road without getting stopped, then we should make it home OK."

Never before, and not since, had Bill experienced such a sight or been as lucky as he had been that night. It became another one of his many nights to remember.

Chapter 8

OF MOOSE, PADDLES, AND PRESIDENTS

> We drove the Indians out of the land
> But a dire revenge these Redman planned
> For they fastened a name to every nook
> And every boy with a spelling-book
> Will have to toil till his hair turns gray
> Before he can spell them the proper way.
> Eva March Tappan

"Celia, I wanna feel ya." Ray said it with a wide grin on his florid face. With a few drinks under his belt, he knew his "wise cracks" would get a rise from his sister-in–law.

It was the fourth of July 1957, Helen and Ray had gotten together with his brothers at Ben's place in South Rangeley, just below Oquossoc. In order by age, Dana, Ben, Ray, Earl, and Archie sat in easy chairs beneath the trees, enjoying each other's company, and waited for Celia's reply.

"You shut your mouth!" Ben's wife Celia grinned over her shoulder from the steps leading up into the kitchen. The cigarette-inflicted raspiness of her voice, somehow accentuated the humor of the moment. "You fool," was her parting comment as she disappeared beyond the door. When the clan got together the booze flowed as easily as the ribald humor. Serious conversation was intertwined with beguiling insults and mock anger. The occasional outsider would be perplexed, unable to grasp a conversation that could change from serious to foolish to feigned anger so quickly. Only the accomplished bullshitter could tell. The women tended to segregate themselves from the men, prepare the food and gossip. The men ate, drank, smoked and talked their endless stream.

Each of the men had their stories to tell. Exaggeration of the details was mandatory but lies weren't necessary. They all, in their own right, had accomplished remarkable things in the woods, and had made memorable rifle shots under the most adverse conditions had caught great fish in inaccessible places, and had escaped the clutches of wardens when game laws had been broken. Stories of poaching and jacking and exceeding the limit were boundless.

They found humor in every word except pain. Getting caught with another man's wife topped the chart along with getting pinched by a game warden for an illegal kill or catch. The top story at the moment involved two acquaintances who had shot a thousand-pound bull moose. To start out it was a bad time of year to shoot any animal, let alone a big male in rut. They managed to load the great animal into the bed of their pickup, cover him with a tarp and head on down the road. There were a few unexpected problems that the two men had not counted on. Moose in Maine were a protected animal. There was no season and any kill was against the law. The movement of some moose were monitored. This particular animal had a tracking device buried in the matted hair around his neck, placed there by the state biologists. As luck would have it, this moose was being tracked on a monitor by two wardens when it unexplainably struck off down the road at fifty miles per hour.

It wasn't rocket science for the wardens to figure out the situation. A couple hours later the poachers were brought to justice. They were dressing out the animal in one of their garages. Their rifles and the truck were confiscated for being used in the commission of a crime. When added to fines and penalties "that moose cost those damn fools something over twenty thousand dollars," stated Archie, who couldn't get the twisted grin off his face.

"And what's worse," added Ray, "they lost their hunting licenses for the next three years."

When the snickering subsided, Ben added, "Hell, if you're going to shoot a moose out of season, who needs a license?"

"Pass the bottle," someone said," I need another drink."

Ben's place was on the shoreline of Rangeley Lake, adjacent to the South Bog. The lake country is tucked into the rugged, mountainous, in the central western corner of the state, bordered on the north by Canada, and to the west by New Hampshire. The lakes are remote and if not pristine, still relatively inaccessible. The Rangeley was but one of four considerable bodies of water, all interconnected. The great expanses of crystal clear, icy water was home to speckled trout and land locked salmon. They attracted the serious as well as the vacationing, occasional, angler.

Ben and Celia had two sons who roamed this country without bounds. Wayne was a year younger than Bill and was an enigma to him. Devoid of any household responsibilities Wayne, during the summer recess from school would pack a bit of grub, a .22 pistol and his fish pole. Disappearing for days at a time and occasionally for a week, he would crisscross the lakes, from one end to another, traveling in his canoe. He would eat what he caught, shot, or picked and slept beneath the boat, living and having fun–alone.

"Celia," Bill asked his aunt one day, "don't you worry when he's gone like that?"

"Na," she replied, "he can take care of himself."

Bill could hunt all day, alone; had even spent a night in the woods under the worst of conditions, but a week? He didn't think he'd like that.

Wayne had a brother, a year older than Bill. Melvin had just finished high school, was going steady with a local girl, and thinking about his future. This would likely be his last summer on the lake. The three boys listened to the men's boasts and their liquor lubricated talk, and after filling their bellies with burgers and dogs, decided to take the Old Towne Canoe down into the South Bog and try their luck. It had taken a while, but fly-fishing had finally come to Bill and he was looking forward to trying out a new rod.

"Watch that pole," Mel shouted, "I've already broke one tip."

"OK, OK." responded Wayne as he launched the eighteen-foot handmade canoe, for a few hours of fishing, before sundown.

"Don't forget the fly dope."

"We're all set. Let's go."

With Wayne in the middle and Mel in the stern, the sleek craft slid silent and swift across the flat surface. There was hardly a wake left behind. The three were expert oarsmen and the cut of the blade barely raised a ripple.

The South Bog was only accessible by water; there were no roads or trails, so, distance from the towns and settlements meant the bog was seldom fished.

The day was hot and cloudless. Glare off the water intensified the humidity and limited the visibility. The Bog area had silted in over the centuries leaving the waters depth, to just a few feet. An acre of lily pads bursting with blossoms covered the areas adjacent to where a small brook ran into the lake.

They could hear him before they saw him. A great bull moose was standing belly deep in mud and churned up water. His immense dished antlers were draped with lily pads and their long stems. He was using his tines to rake them from the lake bottom.

Standing in three feet of mucky water with his backsides facing the boys, the giant animal blissfully chomped away as the canoe silently approached ever closer.

Moose range across Scandinavia, Siberian Russia and North America, extending as far south as New England and the upper Rocky Mountains. The large bulls commonly weigh sixteen hundred pounds or more with their huge antlers spanning distances of six feet. Before the country was settled moose meat was a staple in the native Abenaki Indian's diet.

"Shhhhh." was Wayne's instant response, not wanting to spook the great and dangerous animal into bolting. Unaware and carefree the animal, once again, plunged his massive head below the surface.

"What the hell are you doing Wayne?" whispered Bill.

"I'm going to smack him on his ass with my paddle," he chuckled pulling the canoe even closer to the huge haunches protruding above the waterline.

"Are you crazy?" Mel whispered as he smiled and helped with the paddling.

The great awkward appearing head reemerged. Dripping water streamed and spewed from the six-foot spanning antlers now hung with torn lily pads. The great-wadded beard hanging from his neck gave up its water, like a soggy sponge. He turned his head; white sclera reflected the terror he felt, as the paddle blade struck with a resounding "thwack across his butt." Fueled by fright, the nearly one-ton animal lunged up and away, churning frothy muck in his wake. Simultaneously, hordes of black, parasitic flies filled the air. Deprived of the fleeing animal to feed on, the flying hordes of blood sucking insects focused on the boys.

"Oh, my God", shouted Bill. "What have you done?"

Wind milling their arms in useless defense, Wayne and Bill capsized the canoe as a last resort to the terrible onslaught.

The water was not deep and slowly the three heads cautiously reappeared above the water's surface.

"You assholes." Mel sputtered as he came up for air. "If you guys break my pole…" The rebuke stayed unfinished. "Where's the fly dope."

They didn't catch any fish that day, but Wayne did get bragging rights. He had slapped a bull moose on the ass with a paddle and got away with it. It was also the day that the three of them hatched plans for a trip into the Cupsuptic.

Bill had been working hard, all summer, without a letup. The corn was well up and cultivated. The first hay cutting was complete, and the cow was dry. He hoped to get a little fishing in before school began and before the cow dropped her calf.

The Parmachenee and the little Kennebago Lakes are separated by about ten miles, as the crow flies, Cupsuptic Mountain, Bull Mountain, Bald Pate, and the West Kennebago Mountain lie between. "So, if you plan to make a trip into that country, you'd better pack a lunch," laughed Bill's father. "It's rugged country and it's all up hill, both ways."

"That's great advice Pop, but what we really want to do is fish Cupsuptic Stream and all of those little brooks and beaver dams that feed into it."

"There used to be an old woods road that would take you from the Lincoln Pond road all the way to the Canadian border. I don't know," Bill's father said thinking aloud, "if it's even passable anymore. All those old bridges are probably rotted out by now and besides the last time I was in there everything was gated."

"Wayne said he thought he knew a way around the gate, the one at the main road going into the Lincoln Pond."

"Well, that's just one," warned his father "there are others, all through that country. The paper companies don't want anyone in there."

"We sure would like to take a shot at it just the same. What's the worst that can happen, if we can't get around the gates, we can always walk."

"With the things you'll need, grub, a tarp, fish poles, you won't be walking far. But, you can go for all of me. Your cow is dry, and I won't need the Jeep for a few days. You just be careful, and for Christ's sake stay out of trouble."

Plans were made for around the tenth of August to spend five or six days in the back country. Bill pictured himself as one of the Golden Boys on their Maine Adventure. Where they were going was wild remote country. Benedict Arnold had made his way through this wilderness on his ill-fated trip to Quebec City during the Revolution, and it hadn't changed much since then. The great Abenaki Indian Chief Metallak had roamed this country before that. The Lake Parmachenee had been named after his daughter.

"My God," Bill thought, "I'm looking forward to this trip."

He packed well, tools he would need, and tools he may not need, but took anyway. An old apple crate held the tin goods, and staples like sugar and coffee, to augment the fish they caught.

Bill had matured into a young man now. He carried himself a little more erect, and had even overcome his reticence around young women, at least enough to speak when spoken to. His strong work ethic, a gift from his father gave him a continuing sense of accomplishment. The demanding physical labors of the farm had slabbed his arms, shoulders and belly with layers of muscle and had altered his appearance and dramatically boosted his self–esteem. Feelings that were new to him were being slowly sorted through and given their proper value: his attraction to the opposite sex, his looming future, and his monotonously mundane grades. He had not as yet dated a girl, and this was beginning to work on his mind.

His classroom at school was filled with beautiful girls with beautiful names like Mary and Faith and Joanne. He would roll their soft names across his tongue late at night in the dark of his bedroom. They had soft swelling bosoms too that rose and fell as they breathed and talked and walked. His thoughts were filled with their winsomeness, but they seemed so unaware, even of themselves and the affect they had on him. What was it about them, he embittered, that kept him shied away? They possessed a coyness that intrigued but kept him at bay. A tilt of the head, or the delicate articulated use of their fingers and hands, when they spoke, enchanted him. They stood and laughed with that throaty amusement and sat so different from him. It was best, he reasoned, that he keep his distance. He had no wish to act the fool, and the gulf between was just too great to span.

Nine A.M. on the morning of his departure he kissed his mother, and with a smile tipped his hat to his father. After being forewarned to stay clear of trouble, he started the engine. The Jeep, as much his as his father's, now topless and doorless was packed for a week. He eased it from the driveway onto the roadway and disappeared. He would give up the farm in Mexico for a week just for the hedonistic pleasure of a fish on a line.

The sky was as clear as new glass. The air was dry, warm and flawless. Greenery ran over the mountains, into the twisting valleys and encroached onto the edges of the country road. It was perfect. There would be no stopping until he got to South Rangeley and the home of his cousins.

He altered from his plan only slightly, however, as he rounded the side of Spruce Mountain and crossed the Appalachian Trail. Stretched out before and below him lay the magnificent vista of the

Mooselookmeguntic Lake. The expanse of water covered a million acres of earth. A lightly shrouding gentle morning mist lay in secret recesses. He was compelled to stop. The overlook from where he sat in the open jeep, he guessed, to be two thousand feet above the lake surface. In the far distance he could see the mountains of New Hampshire reflected in a purple haze, and at his feet like a middle finger jutting from a clenched defiant fist stretched the Bemis Peninsula. Far off to his left in the unseen distance lay "C" Pond and much of the ground he had once covered. This was the Height of Land.

Not a house, a car, a road or a telephone pole could be seen; just the green below and all around him. How the Abenaki, who had inhabited these lands for a thousand years before him, must have loved this spot. Nature in all her splendor had really outdone herself, Bill thought, as he took the time to exit the jeep and stand on the precipice in silent admiration. The light misty blue sky, the green-black expanse of the forested mountains and the blue blackness of the lake with its sandy brown ribbon of shoreline rendered a picture of spectacular beauty. No artist could hope to do it justice. He had stood a hundred times where he now stood. He never tired of the sight. Without a watch, he could only guess at the time, but recognizing that it was getting late, he returned to the well-worn seat of the jeep and continued his journey.

The boys planned to stay the night at their home in South Rangeley and head out to the Lincoln Pond Road and Parmachenee at first light the following morning.

Three years ago, Bill had chided his father about the "crap" related to fly fishing, but a lot had happened since then. Under his father's tutelage he had become a fine fly caster and the science of fishing had undergone a change. The science had become art and the art was thrilling. The rig so light, like a feather, so flexible, as to be cognizant, the act of fishing was elevated to a higher, unnamed, plane. As odd as it was to say, he would develop a relationship with his adversary on the far end of the line. Bill couldn't explain it without feeling self-conscience, perhaps a little foolish, but never-the-less, that was what he felt.

Wayne was a worm man. He hadn't as yet made the jump. Perhaps in a few years he would, reasoned Bill. But for now, he wanted worms. At ten p.m., the three took a ride up through the village of Oquossoc and midway to the town of Rangeley took a right-hand turn toward Mingo Springs. The Springs was a tourist attraction along the shoreline of the Rangeley Lakes. It was an attraction for boating, sailing, fishing and golf.

Here on the golf course, night crawlers abound. The three boys quietly moved, collecting bait. Stooped from the waist, holding a flashlight with one hand and quick to grasp with the other, they glided along the dew moistened grass, grabbing the slimy worms before they made their quick withdrawal back down the holes from which they had recently emerged, to mate. The moss and grass stuffed bucket would maintain the plump invertebrates until they were needed. This was the first time that Bill had ever stepped onto a golfing green and was astonished that such a closely woven mat of living material could exist. It appeared more perfect then the carpet in his living room.

Sunday morning as the sun lipped the horizon the three boys, cousins, friends, struck out. In Oquossoc they went on the Wilson's Mills Road for about fifteen miles and then headed north on the Lincoln Pond Road. The well-traveled gravel road sometimes gated was wide-open, testimony to the heavy traffic of pulp trunks on their way to market. A few miles in they skirted along the Lincoln Pond. From their vantage point high on the side of some unnamed ridge they could see the pond below. It was set like a tiny blue jewel ensconced in a baroque, green setting.

Wayne, oblivious to the beauty, hollered, "Stop, I'm cold, I've got to put a sweatshirt on."

"I'm kind of cold myself," agreed Bill, pulling to the side of the road.

"It gets cold in these mountains, even in July," responded Melvin, pulling a lightweight jacket from the small satchel of clothing he had brought.

Several miles further along Melvin diverted his small talk to a more important issue. "I think that's the road we should take," he said pointing to a narrow seldom-used trail off to his left. Not more than a hundred feet from where they had turned, Bill slammed on the breaks, pulling to a stop in front of a sturdy iron pipe gate. With iron posts cemented into the ground, and a padlock, ingeniously placed inside an open-ended pipe, there was little chance of moving the gate or cutting the lock.

Adjacent to the hinged side was a massive boulder, bulldozed into place to thwart anyone from skirting around that end.

"What do you think, Mel? Is this the road we need to take to get us to Cupsuptic Pond?"

"I don't know of any other way," Mel said, responding to Bill's question.

Walking around and studying the situation a flaw was soon revealed in this seemingly insurmountable obstacle. To the left on the latch side of the gate was a number of very tall spindly-branched Hackmatacks. Rising branchless for thirty feet or more, the treetops bristled with clusters of branches, those of one tree intermingling with branches from another. As tall as each tree was their bases were only six or seven inches in diameter. At first glance, it seemed a formidable barrier, with the trees growing at random, roughly four to five feet apart.

"Let's just cut them all down," shouted Wayne. "We'll make our own road."

"I have a better idea," suggested Bill.

With the bucksaw he had packed, Bill cut two of the trees straight across at ground level, creating a flat stump. The tops of the trees were held upright by the surrounding uncut trees. The bases were picked up by the three boys and simply set to one side. With a path, barely wide enough for the jeep to squeeze through, they drove around the gate, alongside the upright trees and over their stumps. They stopped and walked back to the scene of their crime. They lifted the trees back onto the tops of the stumps they had just cut. The cut marks on the trees and the ruts made by the tires were erased with scattered leaves and dead branches.

"And now, nobody knows we're in here," Bill said, pointing his finger at Wayne.

The three howled with laughter, kidded and joked with each other. They were now inside the gate and on their way to fishing holes that no one had been to in a long time.

This was destined to be a great trip.

"Our private fishing hole; we're gated in, no wardens, no competition, no Fire Marshall, no one," shouted Wayne, giggling as no one else could or would.

Once beyond the gate, forward progress slowed considerably. The poorly maintained road soon gave way to no maintenance at all. Small brooks were gently forded and dried gullies with sharp protruding stones were slowly traversed. Chunks of wood and brush were occasionally used to dull their tire slashing sharpness.

This deep into the woods was no place for a punctured oil pan or a flat tire, especially since the spare had been removed to make more storage space available. "A dumb move on my part," thought Bill. Over-grown brush impinged on the trail to the point that brushy tunnels were often encountered. Some could be scooted under, while others had to be cut away.

A hot glaring overhead sun in no way dampened the blood fest of the several species of flies. Occasionally, a horse fly, the size of a quarter would take a chunk, but being the biggest, they were also the slowest and with great relish the three boys had killed hundreds of them, on their slow trek.

"If we save 'um maybe we can use them for bait," suggested Bill, as he held one up for everyone's inspection. "Or, if we don't catch fish," he continued, "we can eat them."

The trail swerved along the western slope of Cupsuptic Mountain skirting the edge of Lost Brook. Crossing the brook at irregular intervals the trail, eventually tapered to a narrow, barely navigable, passage. Rounding a sharp bend, a small clearing tapered down to the brook. Thirty feet up stream a great breastwork barricade had been constructed by colonies of industrious beaver.

Standing where he was Bill could see four great domed beaver houses. These huge colonies, undisturbed for years, had been on a continuous building project. The main dam wound its way for a hundred feet across the tiny stream. As the backwaters grew and spread out, the dam would be lengthened and bolstered and heightened and thickened. The ever-heightening depth of the water would spread until some low-lying gully would allow the water to escape.

The beaver, however, a most goal-oriented rodent, would find the leak, and plug it. The result was a network of dams lacing through the woods that held back an enormous amount of water. In the middle of this beaver made lake lay a huge feed pile. The tips of branches breaking the surface of the water, testified to the enormity of the woodpile below the surface.

"Can you imagine the fish we're going to catch?" Wayne asked nobody in particular.

"No, I can't," whispered his older brother, as he stood at the water's edge. Melvin stood mesmerized by the expanse of water and the height of the dam. As for Bill, he just stood there bug-eyed and speechless.

"My God" finally tumbled from his throat, "Look at this place."

"I'm looking, I'm looking," the two brothers replied almost in unison, in hushed tone, not wishing to break the quiet tranquility.

Whap!! Somewhere off in the near distance, a beaver had discovered their presence and sent out the universal alarm. The resounding slap of the huge, flat tail against the flat quiet surface of the water resulted in a rifle like report that traveled across the water, and echoed off the walls of the low mountains, that made up the valley.

Startled by the crack, the three roared with joy; a laughter that relieved the tension of the trip and the awe of the moment. Everyone was stirred into action.

"I'll set up the tent" volunteered Melvin, "why don't you get some firewood." Bill and Wayne dug a pit for the fireplace. The three went about their chores, each knowing what to do. The fact that Melvin seemed to have taken on the leadership bothered no one in the least. He was the oldest; it seemed natural. Although it was Bill's jeep, and he did the driving, it was understood that the casual leadership would fall to the oldest boy.

The tent was actually a lean-to. A small eight-feet log was strapped to a couple of trees about three feet above the ground.

The tarp was draped over the beam and tacked into place. It was stretched and secured to the ground with several heavy stones "If it rains, we can stay dry," pronounced Melvin, "but if the wind blows, we'd better get some string, cause this baby will fly like a kite." But it was home, for the next several days. A fire pit lined and ringed with stone sat a few feet beyond the tent. By the time Bill had the firewood gathered, the sleeping bags laid out and...

"Jesus Christ. Can we go fishing now?" hooted Wayne as the last of the campsite was put to rights.

"The flies are biting good, I hope the fish are," Melvin remarked, as the two older boys assembled their fly rods and Wayne baited his hook.

Fly casting takes a little more room then bait casting, so Wayne skirted along the brushy shore looking for a suitable spot to get out of the way of the fly fisherman.

Bill favored a Royal Coachman dry fly that he had constructed in the small basement shop that his father had put together for just such business. Slowly, playing the line out as he repeatedly thrust the fly further forward, he finally let the tiny feathery lure come to rest on the flat shimmering surface. Innocently floating, not unlike a mouth caught in a watery quagmire, the fly sat without breaking the surface tension He ever so gently twinked the pole tip traversed the produced the slight movement that resembled the struggle of a drowning moth.

Wham! The surface of the water fractured as the lunging fish took the proffered bait, and headed to the bottom, its tail slapping the water. The long slender split bamboo pole came to life, as Bill flicked the pole and set the hook. "My god this is going to be fun," said Bill under his breath as he shortened the line onto the reel and relished the thrashing pull from the other end of the line. The ferocity of the fight belied the size of the fish. No more than ten inches in length the rainbow trout, though beautiful was not what Bill had in mind.

"I got one" Melvin spoke quietly as he too played his captured foe. "I don't think he's too big, but he's got fight," he continued as he lifted the fish clear of the water without the use of his net.

Wayne, off in the distance was heard to hoot as yet another fish took the bait.

Both Melvin and Bill decided to keep what they had caught for supper but vowed to catch and release until the big one came along. They hadn't gotten started until late in the day and although several more fish were caught, there were no twelve-inch or better "keepers."

"Wayne will keep them all, you can bet on that," Melvin said.

With Wayne's six and the other two skewered on stakes, like hotdogs, the fish were roasted over the open fire. It sounded good in theory but by the time the fish were done, they were so tender they fell from the stick into the fire. In a hurry up fashion Wayne went to catch another bunch while the other two held supper until his return. After that, the fish were pan fried in a bit of oil. The heat would curl the day's catch and turn them black, but they wouldn't be lost in the fire.

When the sun set the blood-sucking insects that had remained hidden during the heat of the day came looking for their supper, and they found it. Constant application of fly dope was of some help, but the best protection was to sit down wind of the fire, directly in the drifting smoke.

"I wonder why the fish aren't bigger," Bill pondered if aloud.

"When there are too many fish and not enough food, they tend to get smaller. I read that somewhere in Field and Stream I think," came Melvin's reply.

"That sounds reasonable," they all agreed.

"Do you suppose that will happen on earth when there gets to be too many people," Bill wondered as he swatted mosquitoes and ducked under small clouds of smoke.

Wayne jumped on that with both feet "just imagine, all these little people running around in little cars." He laughed his open-mouthed grin exposing his broken front tooth. Refusing to let the subject drop, "I wonder how little they'll get. They might have to build little houses and everything."

"Will you shut up," the other two shouted in exasperation. Small talk dwindled down until they each crawled into their sleeping bags, where they found relief from the bugs by burying their heads beneath the top layer of quilting.

Like the day, the night too had its phases. Early in the night the ever-present biting, stinging, blood sucking gnats and flies were busy. They crawled into ears where they got caught up in earwax and tiny hairs; they churned their tiny wings and created an ear tickling vibration. If a mouth hung agape, in they would go or up a nose hole. No orifice was spared.

It was only early August, but the intense heat of the day was repudiated by the chill of the mountain's night air. As the temperature dropped the insects disappeared. The three brought their heads above the quilts and enjoyed a night's sleep. They were occasionally, gently, disturbed by the night's sounds. Rustling in the brush could be heard as the night stalkers prowled the darkness.

Fox came hunting for frogs at the water's edge, the coons lifted stone and rotting wood in search of worms and crawling insects, and the owls sat above the fray watching in the dark and listening for the movements of field mice. His characteristic questioning call could occasionally be heard.

At first light Melvin was up and building a fire. Bill pulled himself groggily from his nest, grabbed a bar of soap and headed for the trickling pool of water below the dam. By the time everyone was up and dressed Melvin, efficient as any mother, had the coffee perking in the pot, and eggs nearly done as they cooked in the deep puddle of fat from the pound of bacon that had just come from the same pan.

"My God this is good Melvin, where did you learn to cook?"

"Thanks, I like to cook; I think it's what I'll do after we get married."

Between mouthfuls of eggs, burnt toast and crumbly bacon, Bill mused aloud, "I haven't even thought about what I'll do when," he paused for a second and then continued, "When I grow up." He laughed at his private joke, down deep; however, he knew that he would need to spend some serious thinking time about his future. He knew he wanted to go to college, but doubted he had the grades or the brains.

"Did you ever think about going to college?" he asked Melvin, as he cleared his mind of his own private thoughts.

"Shit no. Couldn't you just see me walking around campus?"

"Yeah, I probably could."

"Nope," he continued, "my school days are over as of now."

"How 'bout you Wayne?" Bill asked, turning his inquisitiveness to his younger cousin.

"Hell, I'd quit now if Ma would let me." With a pause, long enough only to take a deep breath, "Let's go fishing."

"Hey, you guys," Bill, suggested, "if we don't start catching a few big one's let's move somewhere else. What d'ya think?"

"Sounds OK to me," answered Melvin.

"Me too," said Wayne, "I don't care where I fish, just so's I do." He grinned. His broken front tooth prominently displayed by the gaping hole.

"I hope you brought a comb, Wayne, your hair's a mess."

Wayne brushed a few twigs from his ringlets and picked up a wad of carrot red hair, "I couldn't get a comb through this if I tried," he laughed his silly giggle.

Fishing from just after breakfast until mid-morning, produced plenty of fish but none longer than had been taken the previous day. Melvin slightly vexed retreated to the Jeep to study the geological survey maps that no serious woodsman ever went without.

"I say we cross the brook and go over the top of that mountain," he gestured, pointing off to the east, "we'll come right down on Cupsuptic stream."

"Well what are we on now?" Bill asked.

"I'm not sure; we're either on Moose brook or the north branch of Black Cat. Either way, if we go over that ridge, we'll be on the Cupsuptic."

"It's pretty good size," Mel speculated. "We'll get some big ones in there." He had shouted loud enough so that even Wayne three hundred feet up stream could hear him.

"What in the hell are you hollering at," Bill hollered back, knowing that there wasn't a soul within twenty miles to hear, except Wayne. Grabbing a snack of apples and candy bars, the three made their way around the face of the Cupsuptic Mountain and in less than a mile they came upon the predicted stream. Bill made the first cast and the dry fly no more than touched the water when he was rewarded with tension and a mighty thrashing on the line. He instantly knew he was onto a fish of distinction. It was the feeling that fishing was all about, a jerk on one end of the line, waiting for a jerk on the other end. And when it came, delicious was the word to describe it. The taunt line disappeared into the murky depths, where it intersected the water, zigzagging. The strength of the fight gave young boys and old men alike, a bit of a thrill.

He had known the moment he did it, that he shouldn't have. He had cast from the high edge of a giant boulder perhaps ten feet above the water, with no way down to the water's edge. Wayne instantly recognized his cousin's predicament and volunteered to get down to the water's edge and net the fish, "if you can bring it in close enough for me. The one that nets it, keeps it, right Bill?" Quickly admitting his impossible position, he reluctantly agreed. Wayne backtracked and found a treacherous path to the fast-flowing stream. After the fourteen-inch, pound and a half' rainbow trout lay gasping its last on the graveled sand bar, the three boys circled around, claiming its trophy qualification, and wondering who to congratulate, Bill for hooking him or Wayne for the netting.

"Any fish we catch we'll have to eat or let go you know," Melvin observed, "they won't keep. Maybe Friday morning's catch we can take out."

Cupsuptic stream with its many cascades, innumerable still deep pools, protruding giant granite monoliths and unending stretches of rippling currents proved to be a fly fisherman's paradise. Agreeing to meet back at this spot in two hours the three separated. Melvin worked his way down stream; Wayne moved up stream and Bill traveled a half mile up along the river before he began to fish his way down to meet the two of them.

Having agreed to take no more than two or three of the best for supper and breakfast, they met at the agreed time and struck off back across the mountain to their campsite. Loud and animated they talked laughed and joked, as they climbed the steep boulder strewn incline. Bets were laid regarding "biggest fish caught."

Bill in his greed to catch the biggest had only two fish, after catching and releasing all the rest.

Wayne had four, but no record holders. Melvin had the biggest tipping the small handheld scale at one pound eleven ounces and seventeen inches long.

"You should have him mounted," Bill suggested, just as Melvin cut the head off and prepared the trophy for the pan.

"He won't keep," Melvin lamented as he ran his fingers along the sleek red and green speckled body. "But he'll be good eating," he smiled on a brighter note.

That evening around the campfire no one seemed particularly tired; still high on the excitement of their spectacular day. Melvin, the only one of the three who smoked, was the least effected by the incessant gnats.

"Melvin, have you ever been with a girl? To screw I mean," Bill asked. Exhaling a long thin stream of smoke through pursed lips Melvin broke into a soft, secret, sweet memory, sort of smile.

"Why do you want to know?"

"Have you?" Bill insisted.

"I have," chortled Wayne.

"Yah right," came the, in unison, rebuke from the other two.

Turning his attention back to Melvin, Bill again repeated the question. "Have you?"

"Yah I have," he finally answered in a low almost whispered tone.

"What was it like? When did it happen?" Bill managed to ask, before he was interrupted by Wayne "Who was it with?"

"I'm not going to tell you who, but I will tell you what it was like. My first time with her, it was awful. I didn't know what I was doing, I was scared; shit I was terrified. After the first time, though, it got better; it got a lot better." Then to get the focus off from him, he asked, "Haven't you ever been with a girl?"

"Hold that thought for a minute," grinned Bill, as he jumped up and headed for the jeep.

"Where you going?" wondered Wayne.

"Just wait, you'll see. I'll be right back." After thrashing around in the jeep for a few minutes Bill reappeared, a six-pack of Pabst Blue Ribbon in each hand.

"Where'd you get that?" Wayne blurted in a hushed conspiratorial whisper.

"Where do you think, you want one?" Without waiting for an answer, he removed a couple of cans and passed the remainder. "They're warm."

"I don't care," said Melvin, and then added "Put the rest in the brook, that'll cool them down."

Sipping beer, swatting flies and sitting before the campfire the conversation continued "Now, where were we, oh yah," said Bill, "Have I ever been with a girl? Well the answer is no, I haven't. I kissed one once, but she wouldn't even let me touch her, you know, feel her up."

"Boy, are you in for a treat." Melvin remarked with a broad knowing grin playing across his face.

"Weren't you worried about getting her pregnant?" Bill earnestly wanted to know.

"Well," Melvin paused, the light from the dying campfire playing shadows across his angular face, "We were a lot more interested in relaxation than we were in procreation," he laughed with throaty amusement.

"In what?" howled Wayne, knowing that he must have missed something in the conversation?

"Don't worry about it Wayne," said Bill. "It's adult conversation."

"Screw you guys, I'm going to bed."

Conversation after that dwindled, as did the fire. Wayne still pumped his brother trying to find out the name of the girl that he had been with, but with no answers forthcoming the three retired to their sleeping bags and slept the sleep of the innocents.

In the morning, they ate more fried fish with the last of the eggs and decided to pick wild raspberries they had discovered along the edge of the old overgrown road they had come in on. Any haste to go fishing had lapsed now that they knew they could catch all the fish they wanted, whenever they wanted them.

By mid-morning with their pans full and their tongues scarlet, they turned to return to the campsite, when a strange noise from off in the distance caught their attention. The strange, throbbing, beating sound grew louder with each passing second, and apparently was coming from overhead.

They searched the limited horizon; obscured by the forest all around them, when suddenly a helicopter appeared almost directly overhead. The three boys whooped and waved joyfully at the unexpected sight. Until this moment none of them had ever seen, except in pictures, such an impressive machine. Less than three hundred feet over their heads, the machine seems to pause in mid–air levitation before it turned and disappeared as quickly as it had materialized.

"What in the hell do you suppose!"

"Did you see that thing?"

"My God!"

Puzzled, bedazzled, flabbergasted and a whole lot more, the three put their tongues to many unanswered questions.

That thirty-second brush with modern technology was the topic of conversation for hours, as the three speculated on what they had seen and why. Of course, "why" was the big question? What were they doing way up in here? "What were they looking for?" Wayne asked again. "Was it the Air Force or the Russians?" To break the endless round of speculative questions, "What do you think they were looking for?" Wayne asked again. Bill, in his best straight face, responded, "all right Wayne, what the hell did you do now, they were looking for you, you know."

"I didn't do nothing, they're probably looking for you," he instantly retorted.

The single topic eased a bit as they ate raspberries and sugar, laced with condensed can milk.

This far into the woods, the jeeps radio couldn't pick up a signal. Tired of fishing, they decided to explore a little.

The road, not much more than a rutted path, that had brought them this far, needed exploration further along. Taking the jeep, they preceded north. A quarter mile beyond their camp, after crossing the stream, the road split. One branch continued due north while the other curved to the west. The brook was gone now, having divided into a hundred spring fed trickles.

"Let's go west," suggested Melvin, for no particular reason. As the jeep inched its way along the long-ago forgotten trail Melvin retrieved and studied the topographical map.

"If we're where I think we are we should come onto Black Cat Brook somewhere up ahead."

"This road twists and turns so much, I don't know where "up ahead is" Bill shot back. Within ten minutes, however, small ribbons of water no wider than his arm were repeatedly encountered. Somewhere down stream these trickles coalesced to become the brook they sought. A mile or two along brought another surprise. They ran into another fairly well traveled road but were prevented from its access by another locked gate. "Let's get the hell out of here before we get caught, "suggested Melvin.

They doubled back to where the road had split, the other branch presumably heading due north.

"We've got a few hours till supper, 'Wayne suggested. "Let's see where this road takes us."

In no particular hurry, Bill slowly advanced the jeep over the tattered road that had been made inaccessible by gates and distance. The roads were choked with goldenrod and overhung with brush. This whole vast area was nearly recovered from loggers' mass assault some twenty years earlier.

They had seen many deer signs and had seen the sign and heard the howls of a newcomer to the Maine woods. The eastern coyote, in ever increasing numbers, were making their migratory way from Canada. At night, the boys would hear their high-pitched baying before drifting off to sleep.

The trail advanced for miles, crossing the Cupsuptic stream twice.

Each episode was deemed "not worth the chance!" But common sense doesn't always prevail, and the hair-raising crossings were made. One of the bridges was made up of four great pines spanning a cleft through which the stream ran, about fifteen feet below. The great logs appeared nearly rotted through, and at one end the gravel bed on which the butts rested was nearly eroded away. Still. What good was an adventure, if you didn't create one? Slowly, with the forward winch as an assist the traverse was made. Not without mortal fear of actually losing the Jeep or getting it stuck. They stopped often when the burying was easily at hand or when deep, still pools, like a siren's sweet song, lured them into dropping their lines.

Late in the day they finally turned around, but not until they had reached the head waters of the stream. Cupsuptic Pond was not very big, and its spillway didn't dump very much water, but appeared a perfect candidate for the next day.

"In other words, we'll be crossing that log contraption of a bridge a few more times."

"Oh yah."

"Common you guys," suggested Melvin, "cut your foolishness and let's get going. I don't want to be caught in here after dark."

Two hours later they were back at camp. Fresh trout, canned beans, bread and the best raspberries constituted the evening fare.

"What are we going to do tomorrow, go back to the pond?"

"I think that we should. Don't you Bill?"

"Hey Mel, give me one of your cigarettes, will you?" asked Bill, as he waved his hands about his head, vainly trying to fend off the swarms of mingies and black flies. The black flies were bad enough, but the mingies, too small to be seen would cause the skin to welt and burn with their bite. The aftereffects of the bite would last for hours.

"You don't smoke."

"I do if it will help."

"Give me one, too," Wayne chimed in, not wishing to be left out of something new.

"No, Wayne, you're too young," answered his older brother, as he handed a cigarette to his cousin.

He stuck the cigarette into his mouth slobbering the end into a wetness that frayed the tip. Bits of tobacco flooded his mouth and forced him to spit the cigarette to the ground. Melvin gave him a lesson in drying his lips and how to inhale before retrieving the cigarette. Bill tore the end away and reinserting the other end into his mouth. Pulling a mouthful of air through the cigarette, the tip began to glow, and he could feel the warm taste of tobacco in his mouth, which he immediately blew out.

"Inhale it," Melvin instructed, "Don't just blow it out." On the next try Bill pulled the aromatic smoke deep into his lungs. A coughing spasm from deep in his throat gathered force. The cough did what it was supposed to, expel any irritant that wasn't good for you. The final result, an explosive blast of air that shook the ground he sat on. After a few minutes of uncontrollable coughing and a cup of water Bill erupted with, "You like that stuff, Christ, I'd rather dye of bug bites then live with those things. Anything that does that to someone should be against the law.

"You get used to the smoke after a while."

"Not me brother" Bill said as he ground the end of the cigarette into the gravel beside where he sat.

"Give me a try. Come on brother."

"Not a chance, Mom would skin me alive if I started you on these."

Bill, practically bathing himself, in the oily, smelly fly repellent, "I've had enough for one day," he announced. He brushed his teeth, took off his clothes and wriggled deep into the down filled bag.

The rest soon followed, but just before Wayne was overcome with sleep, he asked no one in particular, "What do you suppose they wanted in that helicopter?" With no one able to supply the answer, the question drifted unanswered. The three boys soon succumbed to the day's exhausting activities. In the late night, as the mountain temperature dropped, the flies abated, and sleep was deep and undisturbed.

A breakfast of fried trout, corn flakes and coffee was followed by a discussion of maybe getting out earlier than expected; maybe late tomorrow. They agreed to fill the cooler with good-sized fish and hoped to get home without being stopped by the ever-vigilant

Game Wardens. Legally they were allowed four fish apiece, but they hoped to double that.

"Do you hear that," asked Melvin. The question directed to anyone.

"Yeah, I can hear something," answered Wayne, his head of red ringlets bobbing up and down.

"Me to," said Bill, "and it's getting closer, whatever it is."

The three stood beside the jeep and peered down the overgrown road, realizing for the first time that they were no longer along. They had company. Around the corner came the army issue olive drab jeep with two men in the front seat.

The three boys instantly knew that something was going to happen. The jeep's occupants were completely out of place for the Maine woods. They wore suits and after coming to a stop and climbing out of the jeep revealed they had wing tip shoes on their feet.

Brisk and all business, the two city slickers came forward, flashed gold shields from inside a leather fold, and demanded answers. "What are you boys doing in here?"

The tone of his voice and the abruptness of his manner raised hackles on the back of the boy's necks. Melvin didn't show any intimidation as he asked, "Who wants to know?" The belligerent tone in his voice gave Bill the courage he needed to stand tough.

"What the hell does it look like we're doing? We're fishing."

Disregarding Melvin altogether the second suited man asked, "Do you have a fire permit, and if you do, I would like to see it?" There was less hostility in his voice, but the tone of authority could be heard.

Bill was not going to let Melvin carry the heat alone.

"Do you see a fire, cause I don't."

"Who owns this jeep?"

"I do," Bill answered showing less fear then he felt.

"Well pack it up and get out of here. How did you get in here anyway?"

"The gate was open," answered Bill.

"You're full of shit, kid."

Bill's short fuse was lit and like Melvin he wasn't about to take crap from a couple of guys with loud mouths.

"I'm not full of shit, but I think you are, and don't call me kid." Bill couldn't restrain himself and rounded off his comments with a sarcastic "junior."

As the hostile talk traded back and forth the belligerent one let his sports jacket open to expose a shoulder holster and its gun.

"You got a permit for that gun… Junior?" Bill asked, returning the intimidating stare?

"Don't get smart with me."

"Why not Wyatt, you going to shoot me?"

"Ease up, Frank," the driver said to his companion. He then turned to the boys and in a gentler voice he simply explained, "Look guys, you've got to get out of here. You're on private land, you don't have a fire permit, and you've got to go. If you give us a lot of crap then you'll have more trouble then you really want," with hardly a pause in his dissertation, he continued. "So, pack up your stuff and we'll escort you to the gate."

All three of the boys had seen the shoulder holsters and the gun butts beneath the suit coats, and knew they had no choice other than that given to them, by the "man".

The two suited men leaned quietly up against their jeep as the boys busied themselves with removal of their lean-to and repacking everything to the back of the jeep.

As promised, the suits drove the few rutted miles close behind the back of the boy's jeep. When they finally got to the gate, around which the boys had so cleverly circumvented, Bill came to a stop. They stopped. Bill just sat there, and so did they. Finally, Frank climbed from his jeep and came forward to the driver's side and Bill.

The gate was closed and obviously locked.

Bill, his hands still on the steering wheel turned to the suit, and sarcastically said, "Are you going to unlock it?"

"Unlock it with your key."

"I don't have one…Wyatt."

"Then how did you get in" said the suit.

"It was open; we just drove through."

"No, it wasn't."

"Just shoot the lock with your gun there, Wyatt Earp."

Bill got out of his jeep and went back to the other driver whom Bill considered the less nasty of the two.

"In a calmer, more considerate voice Bill asked, "what are you hassling us for, we're not doing anything; we're not bothering anyone."

"Look son," he responded to the reasonable question in a reasonable tone. "There's a bunch of big shots coming in here this weekend for some fishing and no one is allowed in here, not while they're here."

"I can't tell you who, but you really don't want to be in here."

Frayed temperaments were somewhat soothed. Bill, in benign resignation returned to the jeep, pulled forward, with just a glance to see if the trees they cut had was still standing. With a little sigh of relief, they were, showing no sign yet of their mortal wounds. Wyatt, with his key opened the gate and watched as the jeep slid by him and continued on down the road. He didn't even acknowledge the three middle fingers, flashed at him, as it went by.

Sunday morning, Bill as was his habit, went to the mailbox for the Sunday paper, bulging with news and advertisements. Blared across the front page he finally found the answers to all his unanswered questions.

"PRESIDENT EISENHOWER FISHES IN THE MAINE WOODS"

"Hell" thought Bill frowning as he read the headlines on his return to the kitchen and his still hot coffee. "What did they think we were going to do, shoot the old bastard?"

Chapter 9

THE LONG HARD SUMMER

Bill was happiest on the farm. There was no need to concern himself with awkwardness, shyness or self-consciousness. His size along with the thickness of his arms and shoulders insulated him at school. Nobody gave him grief. Girls were not a problem; they ignored him completely. He had been held back in the third grade; it was a stigma that had haunted him and had made him a year older than his classmates.

The farm and the woods were where he thought he wanted to stay, but at seventeen, things were changing. His broad diverse reading habit was altering, in subtle ways, his concept of the world. Lately, he had come to understand that the world was a much bigger place than the farm and the town, which he had never been more than fifty miles from. This uncomplicated idea that he would stay on the farm may not be as ordained as he had talked himself into believing. A mental conflict, not for the first time in his life, kept him awake.

There was a much bigger world out there then his own back yard and to know about it only from the books he read just wasn't enough. College and the education it offered was the obvious key, but streaks of doubt clouded his judgment. He didn't know if he was capable of college level work, and not knowing tore at him. Bill finally confided his worries to his closest friend, his father.

One afternoon in early spring, working the chicken barn time together, Bill finely broached the subject, and poured his heart out.

"Don't think so poorly of yourself," his father finally replied. "If you want to go, and I think you should, then, god damn it, go. You've just got to figure out what it is you want out of life." He paused for a few seconds to let the abruptness of his tone sink into his sons' consciousness before he continued in a quieter voice. "An education," he said, "isn't a heavy burden. No matter how much you get, it's never too heavy to carry. If you can get into college, your mother and I will help all we can with the money. We can't do your homework for you, and we can't study for you, but we can help with the finances."

The impetus that begins the direction a young man chooses is so very unpredictable. Whether it's to compete in world class athletics, to climb a mountain, or something as profound as achieving grades that dictate the direction a young life will take, no one knows. But that talk while sitting with his father in a dusty old chicken filled barn affected Bill in just such a way.

Perhaps it was this newfound confidence related to his purposefulness, perhaps not, but his attentions had become captivated by a petite black-haired beauty, and he finally got his first date. As their friendship grew to utter infatuation with each other his gawkiness, began to fall away. He talked with her of his hopes and dreams, his aspirations. She lent him encouragement and shared his humor. She laughed with him and not at him. A close encounter, however, of the sexual kind, one that he was not prepared for, shook him to his fragile foundation. The sexual act, for him, was one of permanence. It was a bond, a pledge of life-long allegiance. Not willing or able to take all those steps, he refused to take the first and the relationship fell away. He thanked that girl silently in his thoughts for many years after. She had seen things about him, worthy things. She had been willing to make a commitment; she had offered him the highest compliment that a girl could, herself. Somewhere deep inside he knew that his path would be long and that he was too young to make a lifetime commitment. He was going to make this trip without her.

"I'm so confused about things right now" he confided to his father. "How in the hell am I going to figure out the future?"

"Well" his father grinned at his son's frustration. "I've been working at it for a lot longer then you and I haven't figured out the future either. But" he added, "think of it this way: Your future is my past and if I had it to do again, I'd get myself an education, and as for the girls, well… You're on your own."

"I really wanted to have… you know… sex with her."

"I'm sure you did. You had feelings for her. I understand that." His father then added with emphasis, "but what you don't need right now is a baby or a commitment that you cannot honor." Father and son continued their work in the subdued lighting of the chicken barns. "If you get into another situation like that be sure and use protection. Too many of you young people screw yourselves all up, no pun intended, by not using your brains."

For the most part Bill's problems with girls handled themselves. Without money, without a car, and the emotional maturity he displayed, girls just seeking a good time without emotional attachment, couldn't be bothered.

For the next four and a half years he seldom dated. The opportunities were just not there.

Bill had come to see his life advancing in a series of great adventures and had begun to collect his memories that way. Each experience becoming a monolith, a marker; a slight vector or turning point around which his life veered. He recognized the simile and admired the thought. He likened himself to the fictional character Anthony Adverse, who wandered through life collecting life's experiences. Bill only hoped that his life wouldn't end like Anthony's. He died when he stopped observing life and began participating in it.

His next great adventure came from out of the blue, as his third year of high school was winding down. He had turned eighteen a few weeks before and was looking forward to summer break. Studying at his desk, killing time actually, until the two remaining days of the school session ended for the summer, his name blared from the intercom. He was being summoned to the principal's office, presumably to answer for some infraction. Misbehavior was the only reason, he was aware of, that anybody was called to the principal's office. Excusing himself from the classroom he made his way along the windowless empty corridor of closed doors and steel lockers to the office of the principal.

Without preamble, he was directed straight through to the sanctum sanctorum. He was being called into the one place that he had spent the past three years trying to stay clear of. Lightly rapping on the door, he entered to a scene of confusing incongruity. Behind the oak desk beneath the great pendulum clock sat the nattily dressed principal in easy conversation with his, not so nattily dressed, father. There were only a few days of school remaining. The principal inquired if Bill's final tests were complete and if they were, he could be excused from the last few days. As they left the school Ray informed his son that he had a summer job. Bill would be working alongside his father and a crew of men in the local paper company.

Ray had by now upgraded the barns that housed over eighty-five thousand chickens to near total automation. Food, water, lights and ventilation were all electronically controlled; even the piped in music, modulated to boost tranquility and the "consumption of grain to weight gained ratio." Man-hours of labor in the barns had been reduced to a minimum. Being a man with no capacity to remain indolent for long, he went looking for work. He found work as a laborer for a contracting firm that had been hired into the mill to construct new pulp digesters.

Ray, as a mason tender and general laborer overheard his boss mention that additional help would he hired. He wasted no time in volunteering his son.

"He's big and strong and he'll work." On the word of his father, Bill had been hired sight unseen.

Hugh Chisholm, on a trip into the Rumford area in the early 1880's saw for himself the waterfalls that he had heard so much about. He immediately understood their potential as a source of power and by the turn of the century the Oxford Paper Co. was under construction. Through the years, it had grown into a giant, producing enough high-quality paper to gift-wrap the world on a weekly basis. Nearly three thousand men and women drew their weekly paychecks from it. Set in a valley at the confluence of the Androscoggin and Swift Rivers, just below the Rumford Falls, from which it derived its power, the factory dominated the towns of Rumford and Mexico both economically and geographically. Monolithic stacks rose hundreds of feet into the sky and belching a constant plume of smoke, ash, and steam.

The uniqueness of the town was mirrored by the uniqueness of the men who built and then ran the mill. In the late 1890's and early 1900's the worlds disenfranchised had poured into the country, settling into towns like this one. The Poles, Russians, Italians, Irish, Germans and the Swedes came and settled into the newly industrialized centers and supplied the muscle that was building the country and the country was being built by hand.

Folks of the same heritage tended to cluster together, no doubt for the comfort of the same language, music, customs and beliefs. Bill was certain that all the mill towns in America, like his, also had their Germantown's and their Little Italy's. In the early years a man walking through the town would hear a half dozen languages and dialects. In time the ethnic enclaves had coalesced and by the late fifties had blurred. Everyone was just American now.

Until this very moment the mill had only existed on the periphery of Bill's consciousness. It had no real meaning in his life. He lived miles away along the Swift River. Occasionally he would hear the horns or whistles, and rarely would detect its ugly choking smells. This intimidating noisy giant was now about to become a major factor in his young naïve life. For the next three months his every waking hour would revolve around hard work and hard-working men. He wondered if he would measure up.

Bill was ushered into the make–shift construction office, by his father, and for the first time gave his social security number, to become a member of the great American work force.

Working hours had been designed to be least intrusive to the normal functioning of the mill. The work crew's day began at five in the afternoon and ended at three in the morning. Bill was assigned to a crew that included his father, which gave him great relief.

Under construction was a huge steel tank, sixty feet across and one hundred and fifty feet tall. A previous crew of steel workers had built the tank, and now his crew was feverishly lining the interior surface with a glass–like ceramic tile. Eventually the tank would contain an extremely corrosive acid along with ground up wood or pulp. The glue-like resin that held the tile in place was special. It could only be mixed in small batches by hand, because it hardened very quickly and that's where Bill's job came in. As the rest of the crew worked on the scaffold within the tank, it was Bill's job to mix the polyester glue that was impervious to the acids and held the tile in place.

Night by slow busy night, six nights a week he mixed the chemical concoction to a buttery consistency, transferred it to a ten-quart pail and sent it up to the slowly ascending staging. His father, worked above him on the scaffold, retrieved the filled buckets and sent down the empties; he serviced three masons through the long ten-hour nights. Other men retrieved the tile from beyond the gate and sent them up to the masons on the ever-ascending scaffold.

It was a great job, and Bill had never seen such money. It was a union job and he was making the obscene amount of $2.50/hr. with time and a half over forty hours.

At the end of each week he was paid with an envelope of cash, which he added to the cigar box on the bureau beside his bed. Each Saturday he would add the contents of the envelope and count it all again.

"You're going to wear it out if you don't go to town and open a savings account," his mother warned him. The morning he went to the bank was a nervous one for Bill. He had never been in a bank and stood before the door not sure if he was supposed to knock before he entered. That problem was solved as another patron walked around him and entered holding the door ajar for him. He was deeply impressed with the stately old bank with its marble floors, mahogany walls, deep brown smell and quiet sanctity.

His footsteps echoed beneath the paneled ceiling as he crossed the room to the brass-gilded cage from which a stern bespectacled matron glared. She counted out the cash, which Bill hesitated to relinquish. Beyond her cage the handle studded, rivet encrusted, gleaming, knob numbered dial, bejeweled, clicking tumblered, steel strapped, massively hinged vault, projected security and safety, for his hard-earned wage.

That summer held a lot of firsts for Bill, the most striking of which was the unending drudgery. Each day began at eleven a.m. when he got out of bed. A big meal was on the table by the time he got to the kitchen. After dinner, he and his father went to the barns. In spite of the automation there was plenty of work to do. Chickens in such packed condition were subject to infections, and it was not uncommon for a poultry farmer to lose an entire flock of forty or fifty thousand in a single night. It had never happened to Ray, and he did everything he could to guard against it. Feeders and waters were constantly sanitized. Ventilators needed constant cleaning and above all water leaks had to constantly be repaired. The machines took care of the chickens, but someone had to take care of the machines.

Both men worked in the barns until about four in the afternoon when they would return to the house where super would be on the table. A quick shower, a packed lunch and a drive to the mill at five in the afternoon followed his day in the barns. At three in the morning the job at the mill would shut down for the day, and father and son would go home for some much-needed sleep, and the whole process would begin anew at eleven A.M. sharp.

Not that there wasn't humor. Bill found the rawness of his fellow workers to his liking. He heard cussing and swearing and fowl combinations of words that defied his imagination. On the early morning trips back home, they talked of the work, the language, and the humor.

"The obscenity of their language," he once laughed to his father, "I should write some of that stuff down."

"You better not," his father warned, "You'll get arrested."

"All they talk about is women and sex. Don't they even think about anything else?"

"They talk so bad about women; I wonder if that's what they really think?"

"They love women," Ray responded, "Hell that's half the problem, they love too many of them, especially the ones that aren't theirs. They fight over them; they fight for them; they fight with them. But they love um."

At eighteen he was still a boy, and the rest of the crew knew it. They made him the butt of many jokes, which he took in stride. He recognized that there was no malice intended. His naivety was offset by his strength, his size and his willingness to work. From the long years of working with his father, he not only knew how to work, he knew how to work with others. Most of the crew were itinerant laborers, gypsies. They followed the masons wherever they went from job to job, living in cheap flophouses, and catching women on the run. They smoked heavily, drank a lot and from what Bill could see had terrible diets.

"Is this what life's all about?" Bill asked his father as they headed for home one warm summer morning.

"What do you mean?"

"Well," shrugged Bill, "All we seem to do is eat, sleep and work. Is this how life is."

It took a moment for his father to respond. "Pretty much," was his only response. Bill sat in quiet contemplation as they bounced along the country road toward the farm. Ray then continued, almost as an afterthought.

"It gets a little better…sometimes it gets a little worse, but that pretty much sums it up."

"Cripes" he almost whispered, "what a bleak future to look forward to."

"If you want better, then get an education." Bill detected a seriousness that he had not often with any other subject. His father's lack of a formal education bothered him and did not want his son to follow in his footsteps.

He began the year with a deeply committed resolve. He now knew what he wanted and more important what he didn't want. A summer of hard labor had helped him come to a decision. He only hoped that he hadn't squandered his chances.

His guidance counselor strongly suggested that his future might reside in trade school. "Your grades suggest that you're not college material," he said.

He had always got what he wanted in life, but he had never wanted much. This time, however, he wanted to go to college. Recognizing that there was not a thing wrong with trade school except being something he didn't want, he made out the application to the University. The application sat silently, undisturbed at the corner of his bureau for three days, begging his attention. Thoughts of rejection fostered his inaction.

"Well, are you going to send that application or not," his mother challenged him one morning in late March. She had sat idly by waiting for her son to come to a decision.

"Yeah" was his only response as he returned to his room to retrieve the envelope. When he re-entered the kitchen, he tossed the envelope resolutely onto the kitchen table. "Send it out in today's mail, will you, please?"

"You drop it into the mailbox on your way to school," his mother instructed, determined that he would do this himself.

For the next month, nothing was heard from the University. "No news is good news," Bill considered. He wasn't even sure he had what it took to go to college, even if they did accept him.

In mid-May the letter finally came. When he arrived home from school, it was resting in his plate on the kitchen table. He opened it, read it, refolded it and returned the single page back into the envelope. As the eyes of his father, mother and little sister looked on in expectation, he simple asked, "Pass the potatoes please."

"Never mind the potatoes. What did it say?" his mother asked in perplexed exasperation.

Without a change in expression Bill looked up and in as dead pan a response as he could muster, "they said I wasn't accepted. Now will you pass the potatoes please?" If he was disappointed, he didn't show any signs of it. He had half expected the response he got but seeing it in print had hurt him.

On a quiet Saturday just after graduation he went into town. In retrospect, it was another day that changed the direction of his life. He went into Dick's Pizza, the hangout for every high schooler in town, and ordered a coke and a slice. At three in the afternoon the place was quiet. A few people were hanging around, but no one he recognized.

"Hey farmer, what the hell are you doing in town?"

In through the door stepped "big Jim" a fellow classmate and football teammate.

"I just went over to the Navy recruiter, maybe I'll go in, see the seven seas."

"I thought you were going to the University." he responded with a more serious note in his voice. Bill decided at that moment to unburden himself of that little deception, "I applied" he said, "but they wouldn't let me in." Then in a gush he completed the confession, "my grades were too low."

"So, you're going in the Navy? What are you nuts?"

"What the hell else can I do?" Bill had been closer to Jim than to anyone else in his class. They had traded barbs and insults, and encouragement on the football field. If he could talk to anyone his age it would be Jim.

"Why don't you go to prep school for a year, get your grades up and then try again."

"Prep school?" Bill asked, "Where the hell is there a prep school around here?"

"Right down in Pittsfield man. They say it's a good one."

"How do you know so much about it," inquired Bill.

"After I got refused at the University, I was going to go there but my uncle got me into the post office, so the hell with it."

Bill poked the last of the pizza into his mouth, flushed it down with Coke, and expressed his surprise.

"I didn't know you were rejected too."

"Shit yeah, you're not the only dummy around here you know." Jim smiled his big broad grin and pinched Bill on the arm.

"I'm just beginning to find that out. Tell me about this prep school."

"If you stop stuffing your face and take me home," Jim grinned, "I can do a hell of a lot better than that. I've got their catalogue and application, if you want it."

"Yeah," Bill affirmed, "I'll get it from you, but it's getting pretty late in the year. Probably too late." Disgust and resignation permeated his demeanor.

"Come on don't be so down beat, if it doesn't work out you can always join the Navy."

Bill retrieved the literature, poured over the calendar, the curriculum, and the philosophy of the school as printed inside the front cover. For more than a year, having set his mind on going to college, the resolve had solidified in his mind. The rejection had more that hurt him; it had confused him and set him adrift. In a desperate attempt to right his boat in a troubled sea. he had set down with a recruiter and had begun to research apprentice programs, but his heart wasn't in it. A year earlier, his father, in an act of studied humor had bought a ceramic figurine and set it on his nightstand. Displayed was a hobo sitting at the base of an old tree with a fishing pole in one hand and a bandana holding his worldly possessions tied to a stick in the other. The message, of course, was quite clear. "Is this where you want to be in twenty years?" And of course, it wasn't.

The tuition, room and board were a staggering two thousand dollars for the nine-month program.

"I don't know Bill," his father responded. "I don't have enough money to send you to a preparatory school for a year and then take a chance that you might not get accepted next year to college."

The State University was the cheapest and the only available option. With his frugal living, Bill had saved every dime that came his way. He now had a bulging savings account with over eighteen hundred dollars. Most of it had come from working in the paper mill the summer before. The rest came from his roadside stand.

"Pop if you can give me two hundred dollars, with what I have in my account, there will be enough. Remember what you once told me. If there are two ways to go, pick the hard way. Well this looks like one of those times."

"Well I also told you, never gamble more than you can afford to lose. You do this, then by god you had better make it count."

"I will, I promise," was Bill's relieved reply. Bill applied to M.C.I. [Maine Central Institute] that very evening.

Prestigious schools filled their rosters easily, so Bill understood the meaning when the reply to his application was resting on his plate two weeks later when he came into the house for supper.

"Ah cripes" was his only response upon spying the return address. There was no theatrics this time as he tore the end from the envelope and extracted the contents. As he silently read the letter his early scowl became contemplative.

"Well?" his mother asked, pausing from her kitchen chores of setting the serving dishes on the table.

"Well," he picked up the remainder of her unasked questions, "they want to talk to me in person. A Mr. Stanley wants to talk to me next Tuesday evening at 7PM." Everyone was quiet, studying Bill, and waiting a further response.

"Heck, it's not a rejection" he smiled. "Can you take me," he asked raising his eyes to meet those of his parents.

Meaningful resolves are not lightly forged. They are pondered and raked over. Life altering decisions by their very nature dictate sacrifice and tests of character. That night and the days that followed, Bill formulated his; to shed the guilt of his failure in grade school; to shed his self-imposed cell of stupidity that he had shut himself into; to shed the isolation that he coveted as sanctuary. He vowed that any more guilt would arise only from his indolence, his cell would become a library and books, and that his isolation would be that of quiet diligence. He resolved to convert his weaknesses into his strengths.

Following a skin of his teeth acceptance, he labored through one of the most grueling, most expensive, best investment years of his life.

Chapter 10

THE UNIVERSITY, LOVE, AND BEYOND

Few occurrences stood above the mundane fabric of his life; the misery of that, long ago, rain-soaked night, under the roots of a tree was one of them. Another was the week of high drama, with the bone shattering twisted cold, and conversations with his Dad. But now, the highest of a few high points of his life, the one that diminished all the others was about to become reality. A student at the university. Until he had received his acceptance letter, in black and white, the significance of what it meant wasn't fully understood. It was the key to his future, not even knowing what his future would hold.

If he had once more been rejected, the blow to his self-esteem might well have crippled him. So much store had been set upon his getting in. His prep school year had raised expectations higher than he had ever demanded of himself; the denial would have crushed him completely.

Summer dragged by meaninglessly with each day tripping over the next. He worked a job at the local gravel pit. He shared with his father the work in the barns, and he endured a few meaningless dates. Prurient arousal flushed his brain on such occasions, but he saw the girls he dated as virtuous. Not daring to offend, he lacked charm and social skills, and his clumsy attempts at seduction were ignored, or worse. A fishing trip would occasionally interrupt the monotony, but his heart wasn't in that either.

What he wanted was to be at college, getting on with the rest of his life. His respectable grades at M.C.I. may not have gleamed, but they proved to him that he could do the work. "So, bring it on!" He would shout in impotent frustration, where no one could hear him but the chickens.

There finally comes a moment in every young man's life when his tread on the front porch step, the latching of the door, even his setting at the kitchen table is done not as a resident but as a visitor. Bill had done these things ten thousand times before. He had milked his cow, and had hoed his potatoes, but the work no longer defined the place, as it once had, as "home." No one intimated the vague feelings of loss nor did he sense an aura. The feeling came from within; it was he who was breaking away. That long delayed moment came for Bill as he loaded an old beat up cardboard suitcase into the trunk of the family car.

From now on, the nest that had kept him warm, dry, and protected, was being relinquished, and for the first-time home would become a place to visit.

Two hundred miles from Mexico, the University was the furthest point from home that he had ever ventured. The quiet drive was occasionally penetrated by abstract promises to write, and to use his time wisely.

"With the money, I'm spending" his father pronounced, "you'd better spend your time wisely, and you've already got a lot of your own money invested."

As the family car turned the corner at the far end of the parking lot leaving the campus, Bill felt that he had never been more alone. He would miss the days of his youth, the days on the farm and even more his life in the woods. He recalled wonderful experiences that others could only imagine. Saying goodbye to his family and friends had been tough but saying goodbye to his hound dog symbolized the end of a way of living for him. He knew he could not live a boy's life forever, but the sudden speed with which it ended, startled him. The farm and the woods had been his home. They had been comfortable, quiet, safe places and he was giving them up for…he knew not what. One thing he did know, his new life would be filled with noisy, busy people.

An hour earlier, when he arrived, he had stood in this same spot clutching the clothesline cerclage of the suitcase that had bound his worldly possessions. Flanked on either side by his mother and father, he had muttered beneath his breath "I hope Dunn Hall doesn't "done" me in."

"It won't his father had promised, ignoring the pun, "as long as you don't forget what you're here for. You're here to learn, if you give them a chance, they'll teach you. Remember, your studies come first, everything else is secondary." His father was still teaching.

Together they had climbed the stairs to the third floor cubical that was his dormitory room. One side of the tiny room was mirrored on the other; desk, cot, bureau and closet. Centrally on the outside wall was a window that look out onto the car filled parking lot.

"It's big enough to study in, it's all you need," his mother said as she ran her finger across the desktop with its fine patina of dust, testimony to the long summer of disuse.

Goodbyes had come quick and now he stood alone with people milling all around him. Their taillights had gone from his view. He turned and left the parking lot and got down to the business of becoming a student.

Lines of young people were everywhere; they were buying books and logoed tee shirts and establishing their enrollment. A cacophony of jumbled words, strident to his ears made him want to spit, but he swallowed hard instead. In spite of the glut of thousands of young people his registration and enrollment was quickly accomplished. His paperwork was all in order.

The long trip had transported Bill beyond his known world into the realm of academia and contemplated theory; hell. Only yesterday he had been reasonably sure of himself, but now as he gazed upon the glut of intelligent faces, it scared the hell out of him.

The year before, he found, had been but a purgatory, where he had atoned for his past sins of neglected study, but there had been a positive outcome. The over-riding contribution of that "set aside" year had been the habit of study; the rigors of habit, and the crunch of discipline. The familiarity of sameness had blended well with the fear of failure, and an elixir of drive was the end result. He had once been told that habits were easy to form, but he found that it only applied to the bad ones.

He was disoriented by the thought of entering this strange territory where the compass of the woods no longer worked. The thought threw him a bit off balance. The only compass that would work for him now would be the moral compass given to him through the years at his father's side. Feeling like the main character in a Horatio Alger book he stood in the shadow of Dunn Hall, his new home for the next few years making up his mind to explore and conquer his new world.

The campus was an architectural sprawl that mirrored changing trends through a hundred years of design, and philanthropic megalomania. Major contributors in their quest for immortality emblazoned their family names indelibly above entry doors of structures that they had bought and paid for.

Since the buildings were not named for the subject matter taught within, points of reference were difficult and his whereabouts became confused. Bill walked the antique brick walkways and correlated classrooms with scheduled courses, judging time and distance. He reveled in his proximity to a genuine seat of learning and in the success of his struggle to get here. Many of the buildings were old but the teachings within, he knew, would be new, exciting and the first steps he would need to take.

Having completed his trip about the campus and solidifying in his mind the daily routes to his various classes. He threaded his way back to his dormitory and the suitcase that lay still unpacked on his bed. Along the shrub-bordered walk that connected Dunn Hall with the rest of the campus he was suddenly abreast a black man, whose intensely black continence brandished ornate tribal scarification. His sub-Sahara accent, articulate, studied, and deliberate, humbled Bill as he considered this man and the cultural differences that he obviously had to overcome in order to be here. He admired the tenacity that he suspected to reside within the man.

"My own battles are enough for me, I sure can't be worrying about his," he told himself as he continued along his path.

Upon his returning to the third floor of Dunn Hall he found the door to his room wide open.

"Hi roomy."

"Hello" returned Bill, to a tall anemically thin boy who stood in the doorway.

"If you're name's Bill," he said as he fumbled with the card in his hand, "Then I'm your roommate."

"My names Pete Coons," he said extending his hand, "they call me "Coon" for short." His "down east" accent was so acute that Bill had to grin as he extended his own hand in greeting. Bill began his unpacking while Coon plied him with questions. "Where you from? What's your major?" and after seeing Bill's few belongings, "yah travel kind of light don'tcha?" And finally, as he breathlessly wound down, "yah goin to the mixa at the Student Union tonight?" Coon pushed aside his possessions that lay scattered on his bed. He managed to clear a narrow margin of the unmade mattress and lay back with his hands tucked behind his head, totally relaxed.

"The first I've heard of it, but sure, why not", responded Bill.

The conversation ebbed and flowed. Pete had two brothers and a sister that had been to the University before him. He had been on campus many times, which Bill figured, accounted for his total relaxation and bored familiarity. This turned out to be the longest sustained conversation he would have with his roommate. Pete seldom slept in the room and at no time did Bill ever see him study. During the first semester he would occasionally see his roommate around the campus, but when he returned from Christmas vacation the bed was stripped bare and all the clothes were gone from the closet.

John, an affable fellow from down the hall would drop by Bill's room often during that first semester. He was from the Cape; Hyannis actually, and never missed an opportunity to tell someone.

"Come on Bill, let's go down to Pat's and get a beer." John liked his beer.

"It's Tuesday night, I can't go out in the middle of the week for a beer. I've got too much studying."

"It'll keep, come on."

"Not a chance. You go without me." He too disappeared at the end of the semester.

Bill was here and he meant to stay. He worked hard and took pride in his diligence, but it didn't take long for the blush of accomplishment to dull as the full weight of his academics began to press down on him. Initially the schedule was above bearable and allowed for occasional stops at the "Bear's Den" a student hangout within the Student Union. Union did not imply unity; it was every man for himself. His father had once told him that an education was a load never too heavy to carry, but he found, that theory didn't apply to the task of getting one. Alone in his room except for the lovely Christa Speck, taped to his bedroom wall, he burned the midnight oil.

Occasional sojourns to the cannons, revolutionary war artifacts that sat in silent vigil, to smoke his cigarettes and brood, became his favorite pastime. Even less occasionally, fraternity parties would allow for drunken relief.

Fall faded into winter, but he hardly appreciated the difference. Penniless and without a car there was no place to go, except back to Christa and her mute companionship. Thank you, Hugh Hefner.

Pouring through some mandatory text one early spring evening at the library, a narrow band of lavender slip protruding below a hemline caught and held his eye. Mesmerized, he dismissed all other thought. Too long dormant, prurient arousal flushed his brain. The silky smoothness of the shimmering fabric and the legs that slid beneath devoured his attention. Hypnotically he stared until a quick hand lowered the upwardly migrating skirt. He raised his eyes to a returning, not unkind gaze. His voyeurism had been discovered, and it tinted his face in shame. By her returning smile of unexpected forgiveness, he knew his thoughts had not been read, or had they? The friendship that developed to a few impassioned kisses was however doomed from the start. Not yet equipped to interact with a young serious woman, emotional ties could not survive.

Gradually the results of his hard study improved, and he could pick out the capable teacher's from the rest. The ones, who thread facts upon a scaffold, tying each together and slowly bringing to life the tree of knowledge. His grades, never spectacular, showed steady improvement, bearing witness to his understanding of the subject matter.

His second year was better than the first, and by the spring of his second year being a student had become a way of life.

In occasional bouts of self-pity, he would mentally step back and observe himself as some cloistered, penniless, ragged scholar or monk. When this happened, he would grab his cigarettes, go for a nocturnal stroll around the campus, castigate himself for his self-pity and return to his studies.

Each succeeding year became easier, as the subjects would meld together. He recognized that he would never be special. There would be no great discoveries, no monumental insights from profound reasoning. He would never be a Jonas Salk, or a Louis Pasteur.

Other than the slow steady gain of knowledge which he recognized and coveted, the one bright light in his miserable life was an invitation into Sigma Chi. In the spring of this second year he moved into the huge white pillared mansion and became a Brother in a fraternal order that he took great pride in for the rest of his life.

He enjoyed the experience, from the initiation ritual of hazing, to the ceremonial induction. The Sigma Chi creed and motto with their high-minded ideals touched him deeply and reinforced deep-seated convictions.

Returning home at the end of his second academic year he was pleased to find that Stebens Engineering, his old employer, was back in the mill building yet another giant digester. Getting a good paying job for the summer was easy, simply a matter of filling out the application. And, of course, there were the chicken barns.

Ray and Helen wanted a little time of their own to fish and play and what better time than when their son was home for the summer.

"Bill, can you run these barns for a while, your mother and I need a little vacation?"

"Of course, Pop, when are you leaving?"

"We're going to take a week over the "Fourth"."

Up till now it had been one endless round of work at home, and work at the mill, so it made little difference that they would be gone.

To his surprise, he got a long weekend off from the mill job beginning the day his father left. After finishing up around the barns he went to town.

By the Fourth of July, Bill was starved for female companionship, and for the first time in a long while with money in his pocket he went to town in search of ……game, any game. Instead he ran into Mary and her University of Maine boyfriend, Dick.

"Mary," he pleaded, "find me a date, will you? You must know someone you can fix me up with," a slight quiver of playful desperation could be heard in his voice.

Mary, with a searching upward roll of her eyes feigned deep thought. In exasperation, "Jesus H. Christ, Mary, think of someone. You're very social. I know you can do it."

"Well, maybe Carol Lee. Do you know her?"

"No, I don't know her–I've seen her with you a few times, but no, I don't know her."

"If I fix you up don't you go getting serious with her."

"What do you mean? I haven't even met her yet."

"Yeah well you know how serious you get. She's not the serious type. Just be warned."

Arrangements were made to have a barbeque at Bill's house the following evening. His parents were gone for the weekend and he was cooking.

At five o'clock the following afternoon they pulled into Bill's drive and out she came behind Dick and Mary.

"Hi," she said to Bill with a modest smile on her lips and the devil in her eye.

"Hi." He took her hand by way of greeting and his mind flashed back to a year earlier. Bill had been sitting in Freddie's Lunch admiring this same girl. She was sitting with some guy he didn't know. He was good looking and amiable from all outward appearance. "He must be her boyfriend," Bill had thought.

He turned to his friend as they sat at the bar. "Joey?" Bill had asked, his companion setting beside him. "Who's that girl over there?" Again, Bill turned his head to nod in her direction.

"That's Carol Lee, I know her. You want to meet her? Come on I'll introduce you."

"Hang on," Bill responded with hesitation written all over his face. "Who's the guy with her?"

"That's Arthur, her brother. Nice guy." responded Joey to the much-relieved face of his friend.

"No, I don't want to meet her now." Then he added, and for the life of him he didn't know why he said it. "That's the girl I'm going to marry."

Joey gave his friend a head shaking look, "Yeah OK."

At that time, there was no explaining why he had said it.

Her look was striking in a way that fit into some fantasized image that he had created in his mind. It was as though, just sitting there she had slipped into an unfocused shadow outline and gave his fantasy vivid features. "Is this actually the girl that I'm going to marry? Probably not." He let the sudden and unexpected figment of his imagination fade, much as a scoop of water drips from between his fingers and is gone.

During the intervening year, she had not taken sporadic moments of Bill's thoughts; Not loud, or pushy, just a thought, not too often, and kind of quiet. And now, a year later, here she was her hand in his and on his doorstep.

She was a beauty with brown eyes and dark brown hair, petite in size and a quick cute barbed remark for any comment. Quick and cute; he liked that in a girl. He was about to embark on another adventure. Unbeknownst to him at the time it was an adventure that would engulf and buoy him along for the rest of his life.

The whole sexy, steamy, thrusting, jocular, sarcastic date officially began with that seemingly innocuous handshake where something, unseen, passed across the skin barriers when their fingers touched, a contact that had been put on hold, that had remained dormant for a lifetime, leading up to this one electrifying moment.

The double date began casually enough over cocktails and light banter. Civility soon fell away, however, as little barbs of ridicule and ego deflating thrusts of rapier sharp wit shot back and forth across the well-set table.

"I remember you," she said, snapping gum as she chewed, "in Sunday school, you were the one with the big feet."

Bill sat for a moment stunned. He wasn't sure what to say. Mary and Dick sat across from each other, grinned speechlessly in midsentence, and waited for Bill's reply.

He knew he had to respond somehow without an awkward inappropriate display of ignorance. The size of his feet had been a source of embarrassment to him since the eighth grade. He was determined to not let her get the better of him in some tit–for–tat banter.

"Why you audacious little hussy, you can make a crack like that about my feet with a set of gams like yours?"

"Hussy! You're calling me a hussy."

"Do you even know what the meaning of hussy is?" He smiled, knowing he had gotten under her skin. He had retaliated but at what cost? Had she been angered to the point of leaving?

"It's the same," she hesitated unsure of its exact meaning, "as calling me a whore, you jerk."

"No, No, No–it's not" he responded.

In defiance, "yes, it is."

"We'll look it up," he offered and with that he grabbed a dictionary, which lay close at hand. Holding the open book in his massive paw like hands, he read, "a brazen, mischievous or impudent girl, it also mentions ill-behaved." He was grinning broadly now.

"Let me see that." After examining the definition for herself she had no room but to back down a little.

"I'm those things. Sometimes," she said, starting with a pout and ending with a grin. "What the hell are gams then?"

"Gams are legs, and you've got a set as curved as fiddle bows, and you dare talk about my feet."

"There's nothing wrong with my legs." He had her on the defense now and wasn't about to let go.

"Come on then, hike up that hem line a little, and let's get a look at them."

Back once again to her coquettish self she replied, "You won't be getting any hem lines raised tonight, so you can just forget about that."

The barbing and probing they confessed to one another weeks later, was their way of testing the temper, the character and the humor of the other. Neither one was able to gain a tactical advantage or to rile the other. They eventually settled into a quieter more admiring examination of each other. By mid-evening the two would hold hands and gently touching one another on the shoulder or the back of the arm. At times, a gently, quick congratulatory, off handed, kiss would be shared during a silly game of miniature golf.

Later, alone, in his mother's car, they explored each other's faces and lips and necks with their tongues and noses. They each blazed with lust and desire. Urges that transported and thrilled were intense with heat and amour. Feelings new to each of them and kept in check only by its newness tore them apart bathed in sweat and breathlessness.

"We better stop," she gasped clutching him once again. This one quick plea did get through to Bill's agitated overwrought brain; they pulled back in unison. They knew they would have time, all the time in the world.

They loved one another instantly, but it would take more time to know if they liked each other. Carol's casual dates with other admiring young men soon dwindled as she made up her mind concerning the direction her life would take.

Bill's return to school for his third year was upbeat. He wrote and received letters almost daily, gossipy letters of daily activities and exchanged endearments. The occasional weekend trip home now had special significance and he made them when he could. Bill's romance was proceeding nicely; he was happier and more enlightened than he had ever been. He had been allowed to peak into another's soul. Carol's joy over the relationship was evident from her constant smile and bubbling disposition. Their compatibility was obvious to each other and to everyone around them.

In mid-November Bill got and unexpected summons to "please come home this weekend," The plea had startled and distracted him from his studies for the rest of the week.

Carol always liked to see him come home, her letters had nearly always asked if he would be able to come home the following weekend. This was the first telling him that she had something important to discuss with him, that she needed him to come home.

It was no small task to get a hundred and fifty miles, halfway across the state, on his thumb. Occasionally, with luck it was easy. A salesman or businessman looking for company to keep himself awake on a long trip would stop. Mostly, however, it was the old feller going down the road a few miles to visit his grandchildren. Ordinarily, he enjoyed the slow steps with its many stops, meeting many interesting characters, but the unexpected summons without explanation bothered him and displaced any sense of adventure that the trip normally held.

The trek home on this occasion was particularly difficult. At about the time he caught a ride out of Orono the weather had turned sour. A light misting, cold, November rain, wet his clothing and gave his windbreaker a, shiny wet, glistening appearance. Not many travelers were willing to pick up a wet stranger alone on a dark road, often in the middle of nowhere. His first ride took him into Bangor and a few miles east on Route 2. His second ride took him as far as Herman, and a third to the cut off road to Damascus. With dripping head, hands and feet he must have been a pathetic prospect. A traveling salesman picked him up, laughing at his expense.

"How far you going son?"

"Rumford," Bill responded hopefully.

"Well I can get you as far as Newport."

Bill found the man to be talkative and friendly and full of fatherly advice. As they pulled into Newport, the man veered into a well-lit diner and insisted that he buy Bill a cup of coffee and a sandwich. Bill had found such kindness often as he traveled back and forth from the university. He never knew what would prompt the generosity by total strangers, perhaps an instinct to help the underdog; maybe just charity but he didn't think so. Perhaps it was simply a gesture of helpfulness that seemed to streak through the American psyche. Whatever it was, Bill occasionally accepted it gratefully. There were times however, when an unidentified uneasiness would prompt him to resist the offer. On one unusual occasion a feller had picked him up in Bangor, said he was on his way across the state. He pulled to the roadside, handed Bill the keys, crawled into the backseat and said, "wake me when you get to Rumford."

Traveling on his thumb was often adventurous, and except for the coffee and sandwich on this night it was just cold, dark, wet and long. Sometimes he would stand at the roads edge for hours, sticking his thumb out as each set of headlights approached. Eventually someone would stop and offer him a lift.

Bill finally arrived in Rumford just in time to get to Freddie's lunch where he was to meet Carol after her shift at 11:00 P.M. He had made the trip in six hours. The hot black coffee was driving the chill from his bones, when he made eye contact with Carol as she came through the door.

"Don't get up," she said as she slid into the booth across from him, without a kiss in greeting, or a smile.

"What's going on?" The smile sliding from his brow.

"I've been thinking," she broke eye contact and stopped to order a cup of coffee and sponge the raindrops from her face, "that maybe we should cool it for a while. Maybe we should see other people." As she struggled to get the well-rehearsed words out, tears began to form in the corners of her eyes.

"What the hell are you talking about?" Bill demanded in a loud whisper that turned a few curious heads in booths up and down along the wall.

Pulling in a shuddering breath, holding back tears, and stumbling along the best she could, "I've got a chance to go to California to work, "I think I'm going to take it."

"What about us?" he pleaded, reaching across the table to grasp her clutched hands. She pulled away, but he refused to relinquish his grip. Tears now began streaming down her cheeks dripping from her chin to the tabletop.

"I'm pregnant," she finally blurted, in a coarse whisper ceasing her struggle to withdraw her hands from his clutch. He released his hold simultaneously. "Are you sure?"

"Yes, it's been two weeks since I should have started my period. I'm sure."

"Sooooo," he drew out the word, what are you going to do?" Go to California and have the baby on the sly; not tell me; not tell anybody."

"Yes."

This self-assured if, confident, beautiful girl, with tear tracks coursing down her face, now looked at Bill and realized how silly her cooked up scheme sounded when it was said out loud.

"You wouldn't just let me marry you?"

"No", tears started anew. "I don't want you to marry me because you have to."

"Can I marry you because I want to? Would that be alright?"

She smiled a pathetic smile, before she slid from the booth, "I'm going to the bathroom and wash my face."

During the ten minutes of her absence, Bill sat and contemplated his future and their conjoined stupidity. Life was hard enough, and now he had just made it that much harder. "Damn it," he thought to himself, "I wanted that college education, but I don't see how I'll ever get it. Not now. We'll have to get married soon; the scandal will kill her mother. Shit, Shit, Shit."

Bill's world was spinning faster than he could keep up. Carol returned to the table. He looked up on a smile of epic proportions. She leaned over to plant a big wet passionate kiss on his mouth. "It's alright now; you can go back to school. Everything is fine. I love you."

"What the...?"

"It's OK, I've started."

One crisis seemed to follow another. One cold night in mid-February, his father's barns burned flat. Trucks, tractors, a hundred tons of grain and eighty-five thousand chickens were reduced to ash. Perhaps some electrical or heating system failure was the cause, no one ever knew. Bill's life took yet another turn, but not quite as he expected.

"Bill, I think you should know that I won't be able to pay your tuition in the fall."

"I know Pop," responded Bill, "I kind of figured that. But it won't be a problem. I'll get a job and go back to finish in another year."

"Are you going to be all right with this son?"

Here was his father worried more about him than he was about himself. The fire had destroyed his livelihood, but Bill knew that the barns would get rebuilt, and that his father would recover. Right now, his father was broke. The insurance money had given him enough to rebuild, but none to spare. The cost of tuition was simply out of the question.

"Don't worry about me Pop," he told his father resolutely, "I'll be alright. It's time I was on my own anyway. You can't pay my way for the rest of my life."

He sat and reasoned it through. He would spend the summer at home on the farm helping his father to rebuild. He certainly owed him that much, and in the fall would live at home and find a job. By carefully saving his money he would return to school in another year to complete his studies. This was his plan.

But that wasn't quite the twist that fate, or Carol, had in store for him.

Throughout the spring, as his studies began to wind down for the summer break, he began to foster a great fear that once the momentum of his studies came to a stop, if he quit for a year, that he would lose his enthusiasm. Would he lose whatever it was that was propelling him? After a yearlong hiatus, would he be able to simply pick up where he had left off? The fear that he couldn't, haunted him. That wasn't the only issue that was nagging at him. He was getting older and beginning to feel the pressure of time. As a youngster, he had started school late, and then repeated a year in grammar school. He had been set back yet another year when he went to prep school. At twenty-three he now was faced with the prospect of two more years before he could graduate.

His relationship with Carol was maturing. They were seriously in love and planned to marry following his graduation. When he explained to her that their plans would have to be postponed for a year, she put her foot down.

"I am not waiting for a year. We'll get married at the end of the summer and I'll put you through," she said matter of factly. "This is not a suggestion."

"Are you sure?" he asked, surprised by her simple solution to his problem.

"Aren't you?" she responded.

"Not as sure as you are."

"So," she continued "you'd have me hang around this town for two more years waiting for you to graduate, so I can marry you?"

"Well," he replied, "that's not the way it sounded when I worked it out in my head."

Bill had never dealt with a resolute woman before but could not argue with her logic. He also had never met anybody so willing to sacrifice themselves on his behalf. She had gone through a prominent Boston nursing school on a full scholarship. She was beautiful, smart, hardworking and in love with him. She was more than he deserved, and he knew it. What she saw in him, he could never quite fathom.

In letters, phone calls, and occasional weekend visits she'd ask, "Have you told your parents we're getting married?"

"Well, no, not yet, but I will," he replied.

"You'd better do it soon."

"I will." But he dragged his feet and he couldn't explain to her why, He didn't know himself. "Is it," he reasoned, "because I have mixed motives? Am I marrying her because I love her or because she's putting me through school?" Not knowing for sure the answer, he was reluctant to make the final commitment.

By the time he arrived home for the summer break, she had settled that problem for him as well. "I went out to the farm and told them myself," she stated with a satisfactory smile. "I couldn't wait for you."

When momentous change is fast occurring, the practical and the pragmatic will often drag their feet.

Tile and Erection was back in town, back in the mill, and hiring. Each afternoon at 3:00 pm, she'd pick him up at the mill yard gate in her tiny red sports car and they'd go for a swim.

"Boy, am I dirty," he said by way of greeting just beyond the mill gate. She fended off his proffered kiss, wrinkling her nose.

"Yah—you are," she responded with a touch of sarcastic wit, "and you stink too."

"Well you didn't have to say it like that," he grinned. "it's just dirt, not a state of mind.

"So, you say," came her swift reply as she pushed the gear shift into first and sped off to in their favorite swimming hole.

They spent every free moment together.

A week before the big day, Ray sat his son down for some final advice, preceded by a confession.

"Your mother and I never talked enough."

"What are you saying, Pop?"

In the dim light of the new barns with thousands of young chickens, milling around at their feet, and pecking at their shoelaces. They bore witness to the comradery of father and son.

"Your mother and I never got along the way we should have, and it's because we didn't talk. We didn't confide in each other. When it went on too long, walls got built. I just want to tell you, if you want your marriage to work, then you need to talk to each other. Don't let things fester." Occasionally he would hesitate, pausing to think. He wanted to say it right. "Share everything with each other, no little lies, no omissions. To just love her won't be enough." Bill looked into his father's eyes with understanding and affection.

Bill's father finally gave the last words of advice on the subject of marriage.

"When you two get in a fight or an argument, and you will, don't go to bed until it is settled, even it takes all night."

"I love you, Pop."

"Me too," he responded. That was as close as his father would ever come to actually saying the words.

Bill and Carol were married on the twenty-eighth of August, a warm late summer day with a touch of fall in the air. The honeymoon was planned for a week at his parent's summer cottage in Rangeley, but those plans fell apart within two days when they woke up to six inches of snow on the ground. It was August thirtieth and the honeymoon was over.

The year that followed was a tough one, held together with tuna casseroles and love. They learned about and from each other. Arguing and bickering between bouts of reconciliation, tightened the bonds that bound them together. She worked and he studied and, in the spring he at long last graduated.

Bill's resume was medioca at best. He had no work history and his grades were nothing to brag about. His only failure had been in engineering physics a course he took as a pre-requisite in premed. He repeated the course, a dumb determination to not be beat. He scraped by with a "D."

With no direction in mind, he searched the bulletin board at the Student Union where available employment opportunities were posted. He applied to several and received two responses. One from Ruberoid offered five thousand dollars a year, and International Harvester offered fifty-two hundred a year. Bill accepted the International Harvester offer. They moved to western Massachusetts whereas a trainee he was expected to learn the intricacies of Cooperate America. There were several young men at his same level, but they soon advanced up the cooperate ladder. Bill was transferred to Presque Isle, Maine. A step in Bill's eyes that was one step below the bottom rung.

It took Bill less than a year to realize he was in the wrong place.

"If you're so unhappy in what you are doing, then what are you going to do about it? She asked. Carol knew how troubled her husband was, but she knew that she should say less not more. In time he would find his way. At this time Carol decided not to talk about her pregnancy. Soon enough he would know.

"I don't know what I'm going to do," he responded in a dejected tone, "but I know I can't stay here in this job."

"Then what?" she asked, not exasperated but concerned. Soon enough he would know that too.

On a weekend visit back home, it was Bill's mother who planted a seed. In casual conversation she spoke of the wonderful care she had received from her podiatrist who treated her for plantar fasciitis. It was this talk that stirred the hot glowing coals of his discontent.

The end of the winter was just around the corner. He knew that schools of medicine would be filling the first-year seats. With a quick trip to his Alma Mata, the University of Maine, he got an address and a phone number for each of the colleges he would apply. As envelopes of applications began to arrive, Carol couldn't help but wonder.

"Hon…what is all of this.?"

"It taken me a while, but I know what I want to do."

"Now don't get upset," he replied, "but I'd like to go to med school."

"How long have you been thinking about this?"

"For a while," he answered, waiting for some kind of a response from her. Bill was a little reluctant and more than a little concerned. He wanted to do this, and he knew he couldn't do it without her.

She stood up, walked to the kitchen sink, and drew a glass of water from the tap. "Well I think it is a terrific idea," she said turning to look at him with a great smile on her face.

"You know this means more years of work for you, don't you?" Bill warned her. He drew a deep breath; the hardest part of this conversation was over.

"That's not a problem," she responded. "There is just one condition though."

"Yeah, what's that?" "When you get through medical school, don't you leave me for some other woman." She said it humorously, but the seriousness of her words was obvious.

As his father's guidance, had slipped away, hers began, Carol's guidance had begun almost as though Bill had been given over for safe keeping; passed from older hands to younger ones.

Carol was his compass, his confidant and his best friend. If she had dreams of her own, apart from helping him achieve his, she never divulged them. An acceptance had been received from a medical school in Philadelphia Nostalgically moved, he thought back to familiar geography and familiar times and blurted a line from one of his favorite authors, "You Can't Go Home Again."

The End

Epilogue

Bill had always wanted to live up to his potential. In the course of his life, if he had become satisfied with less, it was only because he had achieved so much more than he believed himself capable of.

He never returned to Maine except for occasional family visits. He regretted that he could never give his children the kind of childhood that he had been given, but he took them into the State Game Lands where he taught them to hunt and shoot and appreciate the splendor of the woods.

Shortly before his father died, Bill sat and reminisced with him, and relived briefly the week they had spent on the ice of C Pond.

"Do you realize there are a half dozen camps on that pond now. The trail we snowshoed in on is kept open all winter with snow machines." Ray lost himself in nostalgia for a few moments. "The beaver are all gone now. He paused before adding "the big woods are all gone too. Things just aren't the same."

www.ingramcontent.com/pod-product-compliance
Lightning Source LLC
LaVergne TN
LVHW011945070526
838202LV00054B/4800